The Spoils of Ararat

Books by Robert Katz

Death in Rome (1967)
Black Sabbath (1969)
The Fall of the House of Savoy (1971)
A Giant in the Earth (1973)
The Cassandra Crossing (1977)
Ziggurat (1977)
The Spoils of Ararat (1978)

The Spoils of Ararat

a Novel by

Robert Katz

Houghton Mifflin Company   Boston 1978

To
Jonathan Katz climbing

Library of Congress Cataloging in Publication Data

Katz, Robert, date
    The Spoils of Ararat.

    1. Noah's ark — Fiction.   I. Title.
PZ4.K1966Sp [PS3561.A773]   813'.5'4
ISBN 0-395-25702-6   78-1966

Printed in the United States of America

S 10 9 8 7 6 5 4 3 2 1

And the ark rested in the seventh month, on the seventeenth day of the month, upon the mountains of Ararat.

GENESIS, 8:4

An event of such magnitude as the relocation of Noah's Ark must have a particular slot selected in God's eternal timetable. Most biblical scholars feel that the end of the world as we know it is just around the corner. If the Ark is to be relocated at all, it must be found soon. Pray with us, please, to that end.

Tim LaHaye and John Morris,
The Ark on Ararat (1976)

Tear down your house, I say, and build a boat.

Utnapishtim the Faraway

The UGA Memorandums—I

(April 1977)

TO: THE PRESIDENT
FROM: THE DIRECTOR, NASA
SUBJECT: UGA

The following is a summary of the UGA Report prepared by this Agency:

1. The Skywatch–2 satellite photographs indicate that an Unidentified Glaciated Artifact (UGA) at least 96 feet in length and bearing vertical markings is lodged in the Great Ararat ice cap at an altitude of 14,175 feet.

2. Remote sensor analysis has revealed the presence of wood and manufactured materials, notably, *paint, purified metals, and glass.*

3. While the latter substances are not usually associated with the ancients, they have been known and used since early times.

4. Only field research can now determine what is embedded there. Unfortunately, Mount Ararat, lying wholly within the territory of Turkey, is situated in a military zone, and the policy of the Ankara Government excludes the possibility of such an expeditionary investigation at this time.

HANDWRITTEN NOTE BY THE PRESIDENT: Glory be! Let's look into this with a hard nose. Send to what's-his-name at DOD and a copy to RMS at State. Meanwhile, mum is *the* word!

TO: THE PRESIDENT (FOR HIS EYES ONLY)
FROM: THE SECRETARY, DEPARTMENT OF DEFENSE
SUBJECT: UGA

At your request, the findings of NASA's earth orbiter have been reviewed by the Joint Chiefs of Staff and myself. It is our unanimous opinion that in view of Mount Ararat's extreme proximity to the southwest border of the Soviet Union (not to speak also of Iran's northwest), the United States cannot proceed on the assumption that the artifact in question (if indeed it cannot be explained by natural causes) is in any circumstance regardable as a benign manifestation.

It is beyond the competence of this Department to consider the vast theological and social (and thus political) implications the discovery of the biblical vessel would have for the American people and the Judeo-Christian world as a whole. However, it should be emphasized that despite the highly suggestive NASA report there is absolutely no evidence to substantiate the remote hypothesis that we are dealing with a spiritual phenomenon.

On the contrary, all available intelligence would appear to indicate that it is certainly no less likely that the alleged artifact may be of a *militarily strategic nature of unknown purpose.* In the interest of national security, therefore, it is our view that the United States cannot remain extraneous in this urgent and sensitive matter. It is strongly recommended that whatever measures are to be decided upon, presumably in coordination with this Department, total secrecy must continue to be maintained.

HANDWRITTEN NOTE BY THE PRESIDENT: What "all available intelligence?" There's more to this kettle of fish than meets the eye. Give this to RMS at State and get me my Bible.

TO: THE PRESIDENT
FROM: RMS
SUBJECT: UGA

Reflecting on our rather informal conversation last Sunday, I would like to reaffirm my complete agreement with you that there is, as you observed, a regrettable lack of faith among those who are attempting to assess the nature of UGA. Mind you, I'm not saying that the matter should be approached without the utmost pragmatic considerations and that we should not be fully prepared for every contingency, but I found it an odd coincidence that Reverend Frazier's sermon, on this particular Sunday, recalled the age-old truth that mere men cannot hope to fathom the mysterious and ineffable workings of the Lord; we mortals can but serve Him, anticipating no earthly rewards, save those which come from the heart.

However, it would be altogether fitting if your Administration, which more than any other has so admirably demonstrated to the American people its determination to bring to fruition a national renewal of spiritual values, were to link its name for all time to the attestation of such values that the discovery of the Ark would represent. Toward that noble end, therefore, I wholeheartedly endorse the "Open-Mind Policy" you have so wisely formulated, and I can see no conflict, moral or otherwise, as regards the somewhat unconventional manner in which it must be carried out.

HANDWRITTEN NOTE BY THE PRESIDENT: To RMS: Okay. Put this show on the road. We don't want to go overboard, though — the feeling of separation between Church and State is ingrained very deep-rootedly in this country, especially in you-know-which big cities. Remember, my Open-Mind Policy means we're not prejudging, bar nothing, what the Thing is, but we sure as heck are going to find out — *first!*

PART ONE

(July 4–15, 1977)

Incidentally, Robert Ripley, the world famous newspaper man and chronicler of the bizarre, joined the search for evidence of Noah's Ark in 1938. He said he had discovered the authentic tomb of Noah. Writer of the popular *Believe It or Not* series, with a readership of 80 million in 38 countries, Ripley retained an impeccable reputation over 30 years for never being proven wrong.

Dave Balsiger and Charles
E. Sellier, Jr., *In Search
of Noah's Ark* (1976)

One is apt to meet with some very interesting characters in the East.

Frederick B. Coan, *Yesterdays
in Persia and
Kurdistan* (1939)

One

When Tony McIntyre saw the rampant look in the old man's eyes he knew he had made a serious mistake. He had heard in Chicago that ever since the old man had climbed the Forbidden Mountain seven years ago he was not "all there," but he had sent his copies (copies of copies) of the NASA photographs to Istanbul anyway, certain that no other human being still alive knew more about Mount Ararat than Professor Doktor Gregorovius Hoffmann. That much was beyond dispute; one could simply not undertake any meaningful study of the subject without reference to the Hoffmann texts (two of them written in collaboration with Tony's father). But as the frail archaeologist emerged from behind a tower of bookshelves with the ashes of time on his sun-scorched lips, Tony sensed that whatever unpublished knowledge the scholar might still possess would be passed on only as slime to the worms of an early grave.

He had been hiding, poor soul, definitely hiding. Tony, on entering the Cinili Kusku Library a few moments before, had immediately spotted, without however recognizing, the bent figure behind a curtain of flies and dust, his face pressed like a dead flower between the pages of a tome from another century, and now those eyes — grotesquely staring pupils like two spiny plants burned to a crisp on some desert floor — saw nothing but fear.

Hiding from what? Hiding from whom? The library was empty, except for ghosts and a scattering of readers, some of them wearing the traditional burnoose black cape and hood. It was hot. It was damp with the sweat of men and flies, with the steam of the Bosporus in early July. Sunlight poured like molten iron through tall arched windows that had probably not been washed since Atatürk's reforms. Somewhere outside a muezzin chanted from a minaret, calling the faithful for the third time that day. And inside, the dust. The pus of the city. It hung in the sunbeams, asteroids in a universe of flies that watered on the planets of human flesh. It was an awful place to hide in.

The old man approached him dragging one leg like a chain. He carried the water-stained book flat side up, as if it were a slab of stone meant to cover a tomb; it seemed to weigh as much in his hands. Tony met him halfway. The title came at him like mirror writing, and only one word was legible, "Parrot," but he knew it in full: J. J. Friedrich von Parrot, *Reise zum Ararat*; as dying men often do, the old man had gone back to the source.

"Ross?" Hoffmann's voice had changed; it was full of sand.

"No, professor. I'm Ross's son, Tony."

Hoffmann's carbon eyes slipped into the gully formed by a squint of terror. "Shh!" he pleaded, pointing a gnarled finger at the sun. "They are everywhere."

Tony despaired. He wondered if he would at least succeed in recovering the photographs.

"Your father is well?"

"He died four years ago." Tony brushed a fly bigger than the first joint of his thumb from his white linen suit. At the funeral in Saint Mark's, in Chicago, Hoffmann had delivered the eulogy. "Professor, have you seen —"

The old man raised his hand like a priest, brightening in the vacuum of his enfeeblement. "I remember now. You were with Woolley at Ur."

That was true, but he knew that Hoffmann was hopelessly confused. His father had been with Sir Leonard in the last year of the Mesopotamian excavations, 1934, and they had returned briefly fifteen years later, when Tony was three years old.

"I have read your paper, Ross. Woolley was wrong."

Tony sighed. He spoke slowly, in a tone that wore slippers. "Did you receive the satellite photographs, Dr. Hoffmann? I would like to have them, if I may."

"Of course," Hoffmann replied sharply, as if everything that had been said before had been talk of the weather and they were at last getting down to business. He slipped a large manila envelope from the book and handed it to Tony. "They are astonishing. What does NASA think?"

"They're astonished. But I was hoping to have your opinion."

Hoffmann touched the flakes of dryness on his lips and leaned against the bookshelves for support. He tapped the volume in his hands. "He was the first. And he failed. I was the last. It did not bring me closer to God, but it gave me knowledge of hell." His eyes widened, leaping around the room like jack rabbits. Tony followed them; he saw a hooded man wipe a fly from his brow, another shift in his seat. Hoffmann's voice sank to the bottom of a whisper: "They are everywhere."

Of course they were. "Can I drop you someplace, professor? I have a car."

Hoffmann stared at him coldly. He seemed to understand that he was being humored and he stiffened with indignation. *"Melek na'ash,"* he said from somewhere in the grotto of his madness.

Tony looked at him. *"Melek* . . . it means 'king' in Arabic."

Hoffmann nodded, smiling the slit of superior knowledge. "Actually it is Kirmanji. One of the more obscure Kurdish dialects. *Melek,* yes, it means 'king' . . . and *na'ash* . . ."

A black cloak fell on Hoffmann's head like an ink blot. The men dressed in the burnooses were suddenly upon him, dragging him outside, shoving Tony toward a distant wall. Hoffmann's cries were the gurgles of a drowning man. His heels scraped on the floor, making tracks in the dust, until he was lifted and carried away like a hundred-pound bag of onions. Tony, recovering his equilibrium, flung himself at the kidnappers, tackling one man to the marble floor. A knife slid from the man's belt. Tony seized it. But the man leaped to his feet and followed his accomplices out of the door. Tony chased after them, but he had not put one foot into the street when he realized they had vanished, lost in the Fatih kaza of old Istanbul.

The knife remained, clutched in his hand for the kill. The muezzin wailed God's message. Tony opened his fist. The hilt was made of silver, tooled in the image of a snake. Not an ordinary snake, one that could stand upright, and as if it were taller than any other living thing, cast its eyes downward with the severity of lightning. Only on the mountain would he learn of a snake that was the equal of God.

Two

Hakob Meliq Simonian had a scar that circled his neck like a flea collar. It was as thick and as tough as a leather belt, and he was a boulder of a man. A Turkish Armenian in his middle fifties, he lived in the foothills of Mount Ararat, but he was eight hundred miles from home. His cousin had recently acquired a boatyard (in name only, for it was Simonian who had put up the money) on one of the most western points of Asia Minor, and now he stood on a water-logged dock looking from Turkey at Greece.

Dressed in a sleeveless shirt and pajamalike trousers that closed with a drawstring, he was showering under a hose in the heat of the noonday sun, and he could see the Aegean island of Chios, where Homer and the bards were supposed to have lived, singing in hexameter rhythms. Simonian sang, too, without much rhythm but with a great deal of volume, which was his style. He sang until he saw a ball of road-dust rolling toward him from the east, and the words of his song withdrew like a turtle into a shell of suspicion. The quality of being easily aroused in this manner was also his style — one not uncommon among people who live at the base of a volcanic mountain, and in his case it had more than once accounted for his survival.

The boatyard lay on an isolated isthmus, a mere tongue of sand and rock outside the village of Cesme, and its purchase had by design included the few small boats then in repair. Since his cousin had gone to Izmir for the day, Simonian expected no one, and as the dust settled his suspicions were immeasurably extended when he saw a metallic blue Rolls-Royce Silver Shadow, bearing number plates from the Principality of Monaco. It came to a halt by the sea. Simonian turned off the hose. He moved within easy reach of a pile of loose burlap, under which lay a .357 Magnum. This, too, was the Armenian's style.

The man in the white linen suit who got out of the Rolls was Tony McIntyre, which brought a sense of relief (it was unlikely that he would need his gun), but added anger to the cauldron of his emotions, and his suspicion was hardly abated. If anything, however, Hakob Meliq Simonian was not one who often betrayed his truer emotions. Instead, he grinned.

"Ah, Tony!" he cried with a bellow that could launch a sailboat. "You came, after all!"

He threw open his arms in the first act of an old-fashioned bear hug. Tony stopped him cold with his eyes, and Simonian, realizing his body and clothes were soaked (and infested with thirsty flies), gestured a friendly excuse, removing a large colored handkerchief from his pocket to use as a towel, all in vain.

Tony had met him only once before, but he had known of him for years. Tissue-paper aerograms bearing postmarks from all over Asia Minor and the Middle East would arrive in Chicago at irregular intervals, as they had for his father until his death. Usually they advanced a business proposition — the quiet sale of information on how one might acquire (or reacquire) archaeological museum pieces worth large fortunes for mere small fortunes, but always the offer of his services as a guide and a promise to lead him to Noah's ark. "By hook or by crook," was his favorite expression. They were never answered, neither by father nor son, but that had no effect on Simonian's epistolary output, and when, quite recently, Tony and Simonian had at last met, the Armenian finally scored. Interviewing him long, Tony had decided that of necessity they would do it "by crook."

"Do you know the Kirmanji dialects, Simonian?" Tony asked, pulling the knife with the silver handle.

Simonian backed off one step in the direction of his gun.

"*Melek na'ash*," Tony said. He held the blade in a neutral position, showing him the handle.

Though he tried to make light of the matter, Simonian seemed momentarily shaken and this was not lost on Tony. "Aha!" the Armenian said in recovery, "you have been to a Turkish bazaar. Charmed . . . and cheated. A terrible people, the Turks. They would rob money from the brassieres of their mothers if their fathers did not get there first."

Tony prodded his belly with the handle of the knife. Simonian grinned.

"*Melek*, it is a king," Simonian said. "*Na'ash* is . . . how do you say . . ." He pointed to the sculpted hilt. "It is this snake . . . it means serpent!"

"King serpent," Tony thought aloud.

"It is the mark of an outcast sect of Kurds. A terrible people, the Kurds. Worse than the Turks . . . if such a thing is possible."

"This sect. They frighten you, Simonian."

"They are Khenani. You have heard of them?"

Tony shook no, although the sound of the name made him think of the Land of Canaan and the eternal curse Noah had uttered against it when he learned that his son Ham — the father of Canaan — had dared to cast his eyes upon him when he lay naked.

"They practice a false religion. Do not ask me what; nobody knows. They are nomads. But their high-priest remains always on Ararat, where the tribe returns every seven years in a pilgrimage. They worship the serpent. Why? I have no idea. Probably, they have no idea either. Their bible is the *Mashaf Rash, Black Writing*. Their Messiah is Khenan, Zayid al-Hadin — he who went east of Eden. But they are filth, and it frightens me only that you come here. I told you, Tony: no calls, no visits. Not until we go."

He who went east of Eden, he thought. "We're going. With Nick Coronado."

"Coronado? But you are foolish! The whole world knows he is finished. He has not climbed since Everest in 'seventy-two. He dropped his wife. He was drunk . . . manslaughter, they said. You have not heard? It was even in the Armenian newspapers."

"He was an ace. They say you never forget."

"Neither does an elephant. But I would not follow one up Mount Ararat."

Tony met his eyes with the finality of silence. He knew who had gone east of Eden and why the serpent people called him "Khenan."

Three

After the accident, Nick Coronado swore never again to climb mountains, and that included the uphill roughgoing of love. True, in his forty-three years he had shattered more resolutions than a ward politician, but he seemed to be in no danger of breaking this particular vow. With the exception of those six incandescent years with Monique — over five as roommates in Paris and only months as husband and wife in Nepal — he had never been much more than a one-night-stand sort of man, and his passion for mountaineering, in spite of his recognized prowess, had rarely been the equal of those with whom he had teamed, even in the early days. If others scaled great mountains because they were *there*, Nick was not one among them. His affair with high altitudes — and he had also been a steeplejack, a pilot, and had tightrope-walked in a circus — had always been platonic, a desire to be free of a world from which the only exit is up. He had not understood this until that night at 22,000 feet on the southwest face of Everest, and when Monique slipped from his bleeding grasp and left only her ring in his hand, it no longer mattered.

These days, Nick Coronado took his highs from slim pickings smoked, brewed, or screwed, and few people knew or cared where on the globe he did so, fewer still how to reach him. Which was why when a telephone began to ring outside a pink stucco shack on a Godforsaken Sicilian beach named "the Cape of Every Little Thing" Nick Coronado was not expecting any long-distance calls.

The telephone insisted but there was no one in sight, though a hammock slung very low between two wooden poles in the sand suggested that someone might be home. The hammock moved. The sea roared. A hand fished for the phone, unaware in its blindness that the screaming instrument was slightly but irremediably out of its reach. A voice rose from the hammock.

"Shit!"

A one-eyed cat flew out of the hammock. A small, piebald mongrel dog flew out of the hammock. A woman in a faded bikini flew out of the hammock, or rather, fell to the sand crying *"Merda!"* The cat ran away. The dog went to a plate of leftover pasta near the phone and began to eat, side by side with the ringing annoyance.

Nick Coronado dragged himself out of the hammock. Wearing grease-smeared jeans, a torn shirt, and showing two days' growth of beard on his red-eyed face, he stumbled to the phone, muttering. With his naked foot, he nudged the dog away from the plate and put a handful of spaghetti into his mouth before lifting the receiver.

"Uh-huh," he said several times to the unfamiliar voice at the other end of the line. He listened for a while, reaching for an unlabeled bottle of *grappa*, slugging hard to wash down his mouthful and drown the rumbles in his stomach. "I don't climb anymore." He chomped damply. He extended his arm and stared at his fingertips. "If you could see my hands shake, man, you'd — Ten thou?" He reached into his shirt pocket, producing a half-smoked cigarette. He had never seen ten thou. "That won't even keep me in seegars," he said, not knowing why he had pronounced it that way. "Make it twenty-five and I'll stop smoking." He searched every opening in his clothes for a match, to no avail. "Okay. But I don't like it."

He hung up. He lifted the scroungy dog into his arms, the unlighted butt still protruding from his lips. So, he was going to climb again after all; they'll be sorry, he thought. He stroked the dog, uttered his name, "Dobbs." The woman in the bikini — what was *her* name . . . Maria? — struck a match and held it for him to draw on his cigarette, but he ignored her and the flame that danced for the blood in his eyes.

"Noah's fucking ark?"

Until he had learned of the existence of the satellite photographs, had actually seen them with his own eyes, Tony had always felt uneasy with his growing reputation as an "expert" on Noah's ark — as if anyone could acquire expertise in something about which so little was known. In any case, it was Hoffmann to whom all credit should rightly have gone, and it had been Tony's father who had collected and analyzed all the data on the subject, publishing in 1952 a slim volume entitled *Noah's Ark: Myth and Reality*, and one had only to read it, along with Hoffmann's works, to know as much as Tony did. But reputations, like myths, have a way of gathering around handsome figures, the McIntyres elder and younger being such, and with Hoffmann in oriental obscurity, when Ross McIntyre died, Tony fell heir to his fame, not to mention his university chair.

To be sure, while Tony, like his father, had never climbed Ararat, his career as an archaeologist was headed for the first magnitude, and he would certainly have earned a full professorship in his own right, though perhaps not at the age of twenty-nine. Still he was comfortable in his father's chair. His rock-carving finds depicting Mayan human sacrifice rites were considered less a stroke of luck than of genius in that he had predicted, like Babe Ruth pointing his bat, the exact site of the burial grounds from seemingly nonrelated discoveries made a thousand miles away. But the Noah's ark business was another matter, or had been.

It had always seemed to him to smack of a crackpot's adventure, its discovery viewed by most of the searchers as Fundamentalism's doomsday weapon against the heresy of the theory of evolution. It was an abomination to conceive of mankind as the descendants of those prosimian little lemurs who scampered across the earth thirty million years ago, and it was a joyous day indeed when in 1916 the American Baptist bishop Nehemiah Johnson of the Church of God in Cleveland announced that no matter what one thought of man's origins it could not have gone back millions of years since this planet did not then exist. Taking as his source the Holy Bible and the Holy Bible alone, and employing a set of complex calculations that would have made a computer cry uncle, the good bishop was able to show that the entire universe was created on Monday, October 23, 4004 B.C. at exactly nine o'clock in the morning. Actually, the year had been known since the seventeenth century, and the month, day, and hour since the nineteenth — Bishop Johnson contributing only the Monday — but never mind. Thus it was now possible to demonstrate that the first rains of the Flood began to fall on Thursday, November 7, 2472 B.C. (again at 9:00 A.M. sharp), and by an odd coincidence, that the ark itself was a monument placed at the top of the mountain by God. It so happened that a few months prior to the bishop's discovery the biblical vessel had been seen stuck in the Ararat ice cap by an eagle-eyed Russian reconnaissance pilot — then a clamorous confirmation of its continued tenure over 4388 years. It therefore followed, said the prelate, that God in his infinite foresight and wisdom had maintained it so that the progeny of Adam and Eve — and not monkeys — might one day possess the incontrovertible truth that the Scriptures were a divine revelation to man. One had only to recover the ark and that would, dear skeptics, be that.

Even after he had read these pronouncements, Tony McIntyre, like men from Missouri and others, remained unconvinced. He was a scientist, and though he had no gripe against the Good Cause, when the evidence was carefully studied, he was left with only the vaguest sensations. Once, while working toward his Master's at the University of Chicago, he had constructed a chart containing *all* of the significant references to the ark's existence, and it had looked like this:

DATE	WITNESS	EVIDENCE	REMARKS
2nd millennium B.C	Genesis The Epic of Gilgamesh	Differing but similar versions of the Flood and ark stories	Parallel stories reappear in traditions of ancient cultures — 33 in all — on every continent in the world
3rd century B.C.	Berosus of Chaldea	People scraping the bitumen coating from the ark on Ararat, used to "ward off evil"	This is 2000 years after the traditional date of the Flood

DATE	WITNESS	EVIDENCE	REMARKS
A.D. 100	Hieronymus the Egyptian

Mnaseas

Nicholas of Damascus | Wood remains of the ark still preserved | These more ancient witnesses are cited by Josephus (A.D. 37–100). |
180	Theophilus of Antioch	"Remains are to this day to be seen"	In the "Arabian mountains"
330	Jacob of Medzpin	According to Faustus of Byzantium, Jacob retrieved a wood fragment of the ark	It was given to him by an angel, since God forbade him to go to the summit
610	Isidore of Seville	"Even to this day wood remains are to be seen"	
7th century	Emperor Heraclius	"Visited remains"	Says Hussein of Baghdad
1254	Jehan Haithon	Ark visible "at all times" on Ararat	Or at least a "black speck"
1255	Guillaume of Ruysbroeck	4th-century Jacob story retold	Collected at site
1259	Vincent of Beauvais	Jacob story retold	Collected at site
1295	Marco Polo	He was told by natives that the ark still exists	Marco slept here (in a cave of Ararat)
1360	Sir John Mandeville	Jacob story retold	Collected at site
1670	Jans Janszoon Struys	A hermit on Ararat gave him a cross made of wood from the ark	A gift for curing hermit of "serious hernia" (Struys was an amateur surgeon, this was his first operation, he says)

DATE	WITNESS	EVIDENCE	REMARKS
1711	Sir John Chardin	Jacob story retold	Collected at site — always with embellishments
1800	Aga Hussein	Remains of the ark seen	This is what the aga told an early American traveler, Claudius James Rich
1829	J. J. Friedrich von Parrot	Possible grounding place for the ark seen; also artifacts made from a "fragment of the ark"	Von Parrot, working for the Russians, was more interested in getting to the top first
1835–1856	Five ascents to the summit	Nothing seen	Three ascents were Russian-sponsored; Col. Kohdzko accompanied by 60 men
1840	Turkish work team	Old ship seen jutting out of Great Ararat glacier	This is the year of the devastating earthquake on Ararat, changing mountainscape
1876	Viscount James Bryce	"A piece of wood 4' long and 5" thick which had evidently been cut by some tool" seen at 13,000 feet	Bryce wrote: this wood "suits all the requirements of the case" (for the ark)
1883	Turkish expedition	"A huge carcass of a ship in very dark wood emerging from a glacier"; compartments 15' high entered; natives knew of existence for 6 years	The *Chicago Tribune* commented that this "will go hard with disbelievers"; The *New York Herald* said the U.S. Navy should buy it, since "the world's greatest republic ought to have at least one ship that will not rot as soon as it leaves a navy yard"

DATE	WITNESS	EVIDENCE	REMARKS
1893	Archbishop Nouri	Ark seen; central part caught in the ice; "made of dark red beams of very thick wood"	Nouri wanted to take ark down and exhibit at Chicago World's Fair
1916	Russian pilot Vladimir Roskovitsky	Aerial sighting of wreck of huge ship caught in the ice; photos taken but "disappeared" after Soviet revolution	Vladimir said to be an "off center man" but some confirmation given by ex-Russian officer Col. Alexander Koor
1927–29	Leonard Woolley/British Museum/Univ. of Pennsylvania joint expedition	First indisputable proof of an ancient flood destroying a whole civilization found at Ur in lower Mesopotamia	Woolley wrote: "there could be no doubt that the flood which we had thus found (by water-laid clay deposits) was the Flood on which is based the story of Noah"; it does not of course prove, he added, any detail in that story
1945	Unidentified Russian pilot	Aerial sighting of shipwreck partly submerged in Ararat frozen lake at ice cap level	Follow-up Soviet expedition found wood resembling charcoal
1955	Fernand Navarra	Carbonized wood 4' long, hand-hewn and squared, retrieved and photographed at 13,000 ft.	Lab analysis identified wood as oak; variously dated from 2000–5000 years old
1958	Col. Sehap Atalay, Turkish army	Wood fragment retrieved near summit	According to Navarra, whom Atalay later charged as being "crafty"

DATE	WITNESS	EVIDENCE	REMARKS
1969	SEARCH Foundation (a Fundamentalist, church-funded expedition — U.S.)	Wood fragment found at 14,000 ft.	Navarra accompanied U.S. team
1970–73	Various expeditions by U.S. Fundamentalist groups	Looking for highly suggestive "unidentified object" in 1968 photo	No dice; Turkish non-cooperation and subsequent military ban blamed
1974	First NASA satellite photos released	Arklike object seen at 14,000 ft. in northeast quadrant	Imagery analysis questions sighting; more sophisticated satellite photography planned

Intriguingly scant. That was the way he had described it at the time. Hardly a springboard from which to jump to any conclusions. There were certainties, however: at least one memorable flood ("unparalled in history," the great Woolley had said); at least some survivors, human and animal; and at least some children of the former who could recall to their children for later inscription on parchment and stone their ancestral escape in at least one boat.

All this before he had learned of the latest NASA photographs; before he had been impelled to recall that he who went east of Eden was Cain — Khenan, Zayid al-Hadin, the serpent people called him. Now he would have to read their *Black Writing*, and he imagined that it would not be too difficult to find. After all, they were everywhere.

Four

From a balcony overlooking the customs clearance area at Yesil-koy Airport in Istanbul, Police Inspector Nazim Aziz Tahir watched the stream of passengers who had just deplaned from Alitalia's Flight 309 out of Rome. There were no less than a hundred of them in his field of view, but Tahir had an uncanny talent of being able to screen faces at high speed, much in the same way a seasoned bank teller counts a thick wad of bills.

His was a far more accomplished skill, however, learned over time by only the most diligent men, of whom the inspector was one. True, there was also a trick involved, and though Tahir, trapped as he was in an uncongenial bureaucracy that still retained some of the most backbiting Byzantine features, would never reveal his secret, the general idea was to think of an actual screen, the kind meant to keep out flies while letting in light and fresh air. One began with the face being sought for, taken from memory, a photograph, and so on, following which a kind of mental grid was laid over the image in question, allowing only the most salient characteristics to pass through. On the theory that recognition velocity increases by eliminating the variables, and since hairlines, beards, and mustaches come and go, and eyes and ears can be discreetly concealed, one is usually left choosing the always naked, ever-prominent nose.

Nazim Aziz Tahir was a nose-man par excellence. "The nose," he had been quoted as saying, "is the fingerprint of the face," and on another occasion, he had added somewhat immodestly, "and I don't have to dip it in ink." He would be the first to shrink from the discredited pseudoscience of physiognomy, but he did insist that his own work on the infinitely differentiated topography of the human nose was an art. Although it was probably pure chance that his given name Nazim meant in the Azerbaijani root of Old Turkish nothing more or less than "nose," his expertise in that permanent facial erection may have been nonetheless predetermined; his own nose since childhood had been his most implacable enemy. At the age of fifty-three, Tahir had been suffering from an allergy that had eluded diagnosis for half a century. Noxious substances had been isolated and avoided, and even conquered by his unshakable will, but the trouble was that the varieties of offending particles, like the sands, were apparently without number and constantly shifting, so that cure after cure notwithstanding, Tahir was always left holding the bag, or the rag.

Actually, it was his inseparable aide, a young detective named Hikmet, who did all the holding, and at the moment he was holding a photograph in one hand and a box of Kleenex in the other, passing tissue after tissue to the inspector. Tahir, it so happens, was at present being attacked by unknown intruders, they, too, probably just in via jet aircraft from Italy. War though it was, with a nose under fifty years' siege, he had learned to fight the battles routinely, without the slightest division of his attentions — fixed now on screening faces, looking for Nick Coronado.

Had he not been among the last off the plane, Nick would have already been spotted. Clean-shaven and dressed on money advanced in an Italian-cut suit and hair style, he looked more like the old Nick in the photograph than he had in years — though in any case he could not have slipped past Tahir's dragnet eyes.

Moving in a slow shuffling line toward a customs officer, Nick carried a slightly open athlete's carryall bag under his arm, and when it seemed to squirm of its own accord, he tightened his hold around it. He reached into his pocket, removed a small white cube, and taking a quick look around him to be certain no one was watching, he dropped it into the bag. The head of his mongrel dog, Dobbs, suddenly shot out of the opening, his eyes as bright as headlights, and he was licking his chops for more — all to the immense delight of his fellow passengers and the disapproving eye of the man from customs.

"May I see your permit?" the customs inspector asked, turning to Nick.

"I got him in the duty-free shop," he said, smiling lamely.

The customs inspector smirked. He was about to speak again, when two men in dark suits appeared. One whispered something in Turkish in the customs man's ear, and as the officer drew back, man and beast were promptly removed from the line.

They were escorted to a small room with pea-green walls and a barren desk, and told to wait. The men in dark suits took up positions on either side of the door, having nothing further to say. Now that the plot had been exposed, Nick cradled Dobbs openly. He drummed his fingers on the desk, and growing increasingly impatient, he seemed ready to protest, but one good look at his captors, who were about as scrutable as dried prunes, was proof enough that he would hardly get very far.

Tahir, followed by his Kleenex-caddie, walked into the room with a smile that was immediately friendly, though his teeth leaned in several directions. Nick, however, was struck by his nose, which had the skin of a polished apple and reflected the overhead bulb.

"I am Nazim Aziz Tahir, police inspector, Istanbul. And you are . . ." He made a give-me flourish with his fingers. "Passport please." Nick obeyed. Tahir smiled, flipping to the name page. "You are Nicholas I. Coronado."

"The famous international dog smuggler," Nick said.

Tahir laughed three times in hearty Santa Claus bursts. He sneezed. Hikmet handed him a tissue, which he acknowledged by hand only, his eyes looking through the passport.

"American passport number Z one, blah, blah, blah . . ." He looked up at Nick. "I have a brother in Connekticut," he said, mispronouncing. "A private ear."

"Eye."

"Ear . . . Wire tapping."

He laughed three times. He sneezed. His hand went out for a tissue.

"You ought to do something about that laugh," Nick said.

Tahir smiled, crumpling the tissue and putting it into a bulging pocket. "You have two choices. You will answer a few questions before I release you. Or, I will release you after you answer a few questions." He laughed three times. He was about to sneeze, and Hikmet prepared another tissue, but Tahir checked himself and brushed his aide's hand away. He was conquering the foreign devils. "You accept my proposition?"

"I confess," Nick replied sarcastically. "I brought the dog in under false pretenses. I —"

"Your dog will be well cared for," Tahir interrupted, "and returned to you when you leave Turkey." He nodded to the plainclothesmen to take the animal away. Nick held him tightly, as the dog growled at the dark-suited men. They drew back.

"It's all right, Dobbs," Nick said affectionately. "I'll be back for you." Dobbs stopped growling, and Nick surrendered him to the plainclothesmen, who carried him out with four hands.

"Don't drink the water!" Nick called after him.

Tahir drew a deep breath after they left. He looked at Hikmet and his face hardened, but only barely perceptibly. "Now," he said turning back to Nick, "you will tell me about Tony McIntyre, Simonian . . . and the mountain."

The familiar blue cold of glacial ice struck the marrow of his bones.

Five

Outside the Tarabaya Hotel, overlooking the Golden Horn from one of the seven hills of Istanbul, the afternoon traffic was building up to its daily frenzy. The heat heaving from the pavement made the air wobble, and the south wind, the *lodos*, was no help; it felt like glue and smelled of fish death in the distant Mediterranean. It was no picnic, but it was normal, and so, reassuring; the security blankets of big cities are made of itchy fabrics. Something less than normal was occurring inside the hotel, however.

In his suite on the twelfth floor, Tony McIntyre was assembling a high-powered rifle. He had not had much experience with weapons, at least with any employed after late neolithic times. But he had been rehearsing putting this one together and taking it apart again for weeks now, and he could perform with a certain flair. The little practice he had had on the firing range, too, showed the promise of a marksman somewhere in the steadiness of his scholar's eye.

He had always been athletic, with muscle strung like the strings of a guitar. When he had said yes to the archaeologist's profession, his father had prepared him the way a trainer readies his man for the ring. Archaeology was no desk job, the old man used to say; it was digging, and you wore a hard hat more often than a mortarboard. There had been a million books to read, but there had also been as many dawns on the track, and one Olympic summer in Munich where he had thrown the javelin within an inch of the bronze-medal distance. And he had dug.

He dug in Yucatan at Chichén-Itzá's Well of Sacrifice, and when he had begun to specialize in prehistoric western Asia, at the walls of Jericho, and the sixth-millennium B.C. fortresses of Hacilar and Mersin, where he had found burnished, cream-colored pottery simulating marble — figurines of the Mother of Beasts.

He was always finding, while others simply made holes in the ground. In Chicago, his colleagues were beginning to ask in jests filled with envy where he kept his divining rod. It was easy to learn that grass withers first where the soil lies shallowest, say, over the tops of underground walls, and once on the Babylonian plains he had seen by the light of a desolate sunset the outline of a subterranean ancient village where no shovel had turned the earth in several thousand years. But it was more than learning. In archaeology, his father had said, either you had a sixth sense, or you catalogued the works of those who did. Even the untrained Bouchard *knew* when he found in the summer of 1799 the slab of black basalt later called the Rosetta Stone that it was the key to deciphering hieroglyphics, and the romantic giant Heinrich Schliemann needed only his copy of *The Odyssey* and a single glimpse of an immense tract of grazing land in northwest Turkey to break ground at the exact site of the buried city of Troy. The sixth sense was the power to *feel* with the mind.

It was by this sense more than any other that Tony, slipping his rifle into its long leather holster, suddenly felt another presence in the room. Nick Coronado, who had walked the sheer walls of mountains, had come up behind him, and before Tony could contract a muscle, he took possession of the weapon, unsheathing it and holding it like a pistol at Tony's chest.

Recognizing him, Tony was more surprised than anything else. "How long have you been in here?"

"Long enough to realize you're not paying me enough. You hired me to climb. I charge more for stealing."

"I don't know what you're talking about."

"Simonian's a crook. And the police think you're a crook. And they're holding my dog. You have two choices. Explain, or —"

"Want the simple truth?"

"What's the simple truth?" Nick eased his manner somewhat. He was struck by Tony's youthful appearance. Bronzed with tropical sunshine, Tony looked more like a yachtsman than a pen and pencil professor. He reminded him of the beachcombing Latin-lover types one saw in Italy during the tourist season, and he lacked only the tight shirt unbuttoned to the waist to complete the picture.

Tony drew a long breath. "You, me, and Simonian, climbing Ararat to look for the ark. Unofficially, for different reasons, but in good faith. Now put that thing down, goddamnit! It's loaded!"

Nick checked out the rifle skillfully: a 34-inch, gas-operated, semiautomatic Kalashnikov. "What faith do you call this?" he asked, returning it to the holster and tossing it on the bed.

"It's not a friendly place. Now what about this police business?"

"I'll get around to it."

That was all right with him for the time being. There were things he, too, would get around to. The truth was not really as simple as he had portrayed it. But there would be time to go deeper. He picked up a large manila envelope from a desktop. It contained the satellite photographs. He spread the pictures on the bed for Nick to examine. The climber saw the top-secret stamp on the prints. He looked at Tony suspiciously first, then studied them one by one.

There were six photographs in all. Apart from the top-secret classification stamp, each of them was captioned: "NASA/Sky-watch–2, Mount Ararat, June 29," followed by a six-digit sequence number. They formed a series of continually enlarged views of the mountain, the first showing the two peaks, Little and Great Ararat, and the surrounding countryside, photographed from two hundred miles in space, but at an apparent altitude of about 20,000 feet. An inserted arrow pointed to Great Ararat, the higher, glaciated peak. Vertical foreshortening gave it the appearance of a snowball splattered on a dirty windowpane.

The second, third, fourth, and fifth photographs were all of Great Ararat, each a one hundred percent enlargement of the previous one.

In photograph two, a point near the very top was circled, and a red mark of indiscriminate shape lay within the circle. This was labeled "iron." In photograph three, a distinct bulge could be seen in the ice cap. A yellow spot appeared beside the red, labeled "glass." The fourth blowup showed fuzzy, but clearly vertical lines in the bulge. A blue spot, "paint," joined the others. The fifth and most magnified print revealed the markings in the bulge more prominently, though still unidentifiably. Another spot, bright orange, was called simply "other metals (unidentified)."

The sixth and final photograph was a duplicate of the fifth, except that a small drawing had been superimposed over the bulge in the mountain. It was an artist's rendering of Noah's ark, drawn to scale on the basis of the dimensions given in the Bible. All of the colored spots fell within the outlines of the boat.

There had been a long, puzzling rustling sound on Tahir's lately installed bugging machine down the hall, but the inspector had waited patiently, and now Tony's voice took command of the speaker.

"That's not your everyday garden variety of coincidence," Tony said, and Tahir looked at Hikmet and shrugged.

"You forgot about two simple truths," Nick was heard to reply. "Nobody climbs Ararat without entering the military zone. And no one who wants to climb enters. There's a missile base there, and they've got a thing about spies. Do you know what they do to 'spies' in this country?"

Tahir smiled.

"Simonian knows the area without bringing the Turks down on us," Tony's voice responded.

"Simonian!" Tahir interjected. "Always Simonian! I will get him!"

Hikmet nodded.

"So he's a small-time crook," Tony continued, moving about the bugged suite, "but he can't steal the ark. What's the second thing?"

"There's no fucking ark, that's what . . . Maybe there's something up there, but the satellite found metals, paint, glass. The ark was made of wood, in case you didn't know."

Tony stood tall with authority. "Gopherwood, which was really cypress, according to my reading of the Greek and Hebrew texts. Ribs of cypress, covered with reeds, and coated inside and out with pitch. Length, four hundred and fifty feet; width, seventy-five; height, forty-five, with an eighteen-inch fall to the roof. Three decks, a little window and a door on the side. Lots of crude *iron* nails, beeswax *paint*, and fused silica *glass*. That's Noah's ark . . . and I know where it is." He was surprised to hear himself speak so categorically. A few months back, he would have sounded to his own ears like the crackpots. But the crackpots had never seen the photographs taken by Skywatch–2.

"Where'd you get these pictures, anyway?" Nick asked staring at Tony oddly. "It says here they're secret."

"I'm rich. *Very* rich, Nick. I can afford things other people can't."

Nick scowled. He was about to say something to express his doubt that one could simply purchase U.S. government secrets, not to mention the Soviet-made Kalashnikov, though he was not someone who believed the rich were no different from himself. He might have just dropped the matter with a stinging "Rich kid!" but an urgent knocking at the door stopped him short of uttering anything at all. Instead, he turned to Tony, who suddenly appeared to take fright.

It was not the knocking of knuckle on wood, but something a great deal more intrusive. The wood splintered. The blade of an ax smashed through. The door flew open. Four black-hooded men charged into the room swinging as many axes for the kill.

Nick dove for the Kalashnikov, firing blindly through the holster at one of them who was about to decapitate Tony. The man blew out like an electric bulb, but his ax still had plenty of spunk and it took off for the stars, though it was stopped by the ceiling, where it hung by its blade in the plaster.

Nick got off another wild shot that went nowhere, and when he tried to use the rifle to block an ax swing meant to widen his navel, it saved him, but the weapon flew from his hands.

Tony had grabbed the ax stuck in the ceiling, and holding off the three silent killers momentarily, while they assumed a new line of attack, both Nick and Tony were able to retreat into the corridor.

One of the axmen took after Nick, who in a hairline of time was compelled to make a fateful decision: he had no doubt that he could outrun the overly cloaked axman; even on bad days he could fly, and now it was all downhill; probably the axman would not even try to pursue him, but he had already come between Nick and Tony, and Nick's flight would leave Tony surrounded and, very shortly, definitely dead. So what? he thought. But there was twenty-five thou at stake. And climbing the mountain. That was it, the mountain, of all things, the clincher. Nick, instead of running, as the axman expected, did a sharp reverse and rushed him.

The axman sliced air like a fan, but a backhanded chop at his forearm separated the ax from the man. They locked, gnashing like gears going two different ways. The man drew a knife. Their matched strength struck a crushing balance, and they buckled, falling slowly, not to the floor, but into an open laundry dumbwaiter, and they disappeared, sinking, spilling blood.

Tony was alone, two axes to one. He could feel wind ruffling his hair as he ducked a swipe at his face, but a maid, turning the corridor corner with more sheets for the laundry chute, took it head on. The neck, to be precise. The blade sank as far as the cervical vertebrae, which are what hold it all in place. The head went up like the top of a beer stein. It didn't quite fall off; it hung on her back, her ears in her armpits.

The next one had Tony's name on it. Tony swung, too, catching it on the fly in the handle, lopping off the axman's blade and leaving him with only a stump of a club, hardly enough to swat flies. Tony spun full circle, coming around with another swing and slamming the axman's skull on the bridge of his nose. The bridge collapsed. The blade took his eyes and his forehead and part of his scalp, slicing through in a drizzle of brain splatter, but the last remaining axman already had another blade airborne, and Tony, who was still coming out of his turn, had not yet begun to dodge. Like an outfielder judging a long fly ball, he knew where it would land, and he thought, Shit, my teeth!

But the axman died instead. He dropped to the floor, going down like a corkscrew, launching his ax into purposeless flight, crumbling in a blast of light and sound.

Tony wheeled in the direction of the gunfire. A man with a shiny nose stood halfway down the hall holding a pistol in his hand. Another man was beside him holding a box of Kleenex. Shiny-nose had one of the friendliest smiles Tony had ever seen, and when he bowed deeply in the old-European manner, Tony grinned and half-saluted, then turned and ran looking for Nick.

The dumbwaiter arrived in the laundry room with red sheets and redder puddles. Some hotels may have red sheets, and, as every hotel laundry worker knows, all have sheets occasionally stained with blood, but none have red puddles. Which was why the basement crew, who had been waiting too long for a signal from the twelfth-floor maid and had decided to pull down the dumbwaiter anyway, knew they were dealing with a special case. All the more so when it began to stir, revealing two human bodies inside, one of them eyes-agape dead.

Drenched in the axman's blood, Nick climbed out of the dumbwaiter like a resurrection, as Tony came rushing into the room. The workmen, who had been washing linens all day, stood frozen in various degrees of wetness, most of it fear-sweat, but Tony was visibly pleased to see Nick whole and erect, though badly in need of water, soap, and a towel.

"You sure came to the right place," Tony said smiling even more broadly than he had for Shiny-nose.

Nick, however, failed to appreciate Tony's good humor, considering the circumstances. His mouth tasted of the axman's last breath and he was understandably livid.

"You listen to me, rich kid!" he cried. "I'm poor. I want Swiss francs. I want them all in advance." He began to remove his bloody clothes. "I want . . . I want a new shirt. In advance! I want a goddamn explanation of what this is all about. In fucking advance! And I don't want, I *don't* want, ever again to hear the words 'Noah's ark'!"

He tossed his shirt to one of the laundrymen, apparently the chief, because when the others looked at him bewilderedly, he shoved the garment into a mere flunky's hands and shouted at him in a kind of English: "He say, he don't want 'no-a starch'!"

The real cleanup had been left to Nazim Aziz Tahir. Without their knowledge, he had by craft allowed Nick and Tony to depart from the grisly scene before beginning his investigation, but it had been long and customarily thorough. Now, much later that evening, he sat in his upholstered inspector's chair — the prize of the number one man — studying the knife with the serpent handle that Nick had used to kill his hooded axman.

He sneezed, and when Hikmet, perhaps due to the late hour, failed to produce a tissue, Tahir grew irascible, jabbing an angry thumb at a row of potted plants on his desk.

"I am allergic to all of them!"

Hikmet, wondering how they had gotten there in the first place, began to remove them, but Tahir stopped him.

"No. I must fight them!" He got up and paced, touching the configurations of his nose with weightless fingers, delving into the case. "Should we inform Ankara?" he asked Hikmet.

Hikmet tried to stammer a reply, but before he could gather up a word, Tahir interrupted.

"You are right," he said, his mouth then turning down in mighty derogation. "They would arrest them at once as 'spies' ... as if secrets can be kept secret in Turkey." Tahir tried another approach. "So, they have fallen into Simonian's trap." His fingers danced on his nose like Nureyev, but they took an abstract form of a gun when he turned to Hikmet and pointed a .38 caliber reminder. "I will get him!"

Hikmet made an attempt to stutter advice. Hikmet not only stammered, he stuttered. Tahir intervened.

"You are right. We must play Simonian's game, to learn what it is."

Hikmet, in the flush of self-pride (he was not always so right), added another try. Tahir smiled paternally and patted the young detective on his back.

"Yes. Yes. There is time. Let them climb the mountain. As the Americans say, 'Whatever goes up, must come down.'"

Hikmet nodded slowly in a flawless impersonation of what

Tahir was doing at that moment, then he picked up the serpent knife and looked at Tahir with a question.

Tahir shrugged, having no knowledge of what it might signify, but that did not mean he was not concerned, and his voice was resonant with the sound of wisdom, when, after a few turns on his skating-rink nose, he said, "There is time."

Six

Tony realized at once that he had said the wrong thing. They were in the Rolls-Royce, Tony at the wheel, Nick alongside, crossing the new bridge over the Bosporus that links Europe to Asia Minor, and he had been unable to erase the image of the hooded man's head being whittled like wood for kindling, but it had been gratuitous, if not unkind, to say to someone who felt responsible for his own wife's death, "I never killed anyone before."

"Really?" Nick said cuttingly. "In South Philly, where I come from, you start real early. And if you can't make it on your own, your old man takes you the first time."

He fell silent, and Tony let the matter burn down like an ember. It had been going fine for a while, in a businesslike way. They had had dinner together the night before, and Nick's mood, lightened by a bottle of *raki*, had been almost pleasant. He had recounted his experience with Tahir: how he had denied everything, and how at a certain point Tahir had allowed him to go with a simple warning to stay away from the mountain, reminding him that he had his dog as a hostage. From Nick's story, Tony was sure that Tahir and Shiny-nose were one and the same, but he had said nothing to Nick, and in any case, they agreed that once gone from Istanbul they would be beyond local police jurisdiction. Tony had told him about the serpent people, theorizing that their display of violence had something to do with the Hoffmann kidnapping, which he said he could not explain. But outside of Istanbul, he had reasoned once more, there would seem to be no cause to believe that they would encounter such serious trouble again. Nick had shown scarce interest in discussing the affair, and Tony, preferring to keep it that way, had failed to mention the serpent people's septennial pilgrimages to Ararat, and that since Hoffmann had been there in 1970, this was undoubtedly a seventh year.

They were on the Asian continent, heading south down the coast road, when Nick spoke again. The windows were open and the sea winds had softened his face, and he was breaking the seal on the kind of metal box that comes with only the most important cigars.

"As long as we're looking for Bible-story props," he said with a half-smile on his lips, "it'd be a lot more fun finding the Garden of Eden. Or was that on top of a mountain, too, professor?"

Tony shook no, delighted that the tension had eased. "But it was in Turkey."

Nick turned to him. He had never heard that one before. "Now how the hell do you know that? I suppose you've already discovered it, or maybe just a couple of fossilized apples."

Tony smiled. Nick was needling, but in a friendly way, for a change, and he had actually called him "professor." "It's all in the Bible, Nick. The only other thing you need is a map. There was a river that ran through Eden. It broke up into four streams, two of them with names that no longer exist, but the others were the Tigris and the Euphrates. So the only place the garden could have been —" He suddenly broke his sentence, startled by a shaft of insight, as a mental picture of the geographical site unfolded before his eyes. ". . . was in central Turkey," he finished slowly . . . "I just thought of something: you know what lies due east of Eden?"

"Let me guess. Wonderland? No, Oz."

"No, Ararat."

"So does Japan. What does it mean?"

"I don't know," Tony said thoughtfully.

"Don't worry, kid, you'll dream it up." Nick sat back in the leather seat. He removed the cellophane wrapping from a Partagas, moistened both ends of the cigar, and lit it carefully with a stick match. "You know," he said relishing the smoke, "when you climb Everest, everyone with you has always got his eyes peeled for the Abominable Snowman. Well, there's a joke that inevitably makes the rounds on that hill: There's this climber from Texas who finally comes face to face with the thing, a giant of a creature covered with snow. And the Texan is scared shitless, and he yells out, 'The Abominable Snowman!' And the fucking monster looks at him real wide-eyed, even more scared than him, and he shouts, 'Where? Where?'" Nick waited for Tony's smile, then he drew deeply on his Havana, and went on. "That's the trouble with you guys. Always reading into things, making them bigger than they are. I'll bet if old Jesus came down, and someone yelled, 'There's Christ!' He'd drop to his knees making a cross." Nick blew a thin blue line of smoke. "Now wouldn't that be a kick in Christianity's ass?"

A decrepit old power launch, newly rechristened the *Oskedar*, bobbed in the boatyard waters. Simonian stood on the dock watching his cousin unload supplies from the boat — cans of high-octane gasoline, camping equipment, mountaineering irons, canned foods, and cordage — everything recently purchased in Cyprus and flown illicitly to a nearby tobacco field during the previous night. Simonian's cousin, a bent twig of a man named Papazian, was doing all the work by himself, while Simonian, his arms lying across his chest like two sleeping cobras, supervised, taking the sun, casting an enormous shadow.

The Rolls-Royce came out of the dust, and when Simonian saw it nearing, he waved and broke into a grin as wide as the slot on a mailbox. Holding his smile in the vise of his facial muscles, he spoke fire to Papazian.

"They are here. I will be back on the twenty-second."

"You must," said Papazian, his hunched-over body a mirror of sweat. "They will not wait."

"We have waited thirty-two years. They will wait."

Nick and Tony got out of the Rolls. Simonian, stepping over a tangle of fishing nets, rushed up to Tony and embraced him. Papazian opened the trunk of the car and began to load it. Tony started to introduce Simonian to Nick, but the Armenian bearhugged him like an old uncle, though they had never met before. Nick tightened his arms and his back, erecting a wall against the lavish greeting.

"Mister Coronado!" Simonian sang in an ear-shaking basso pretending not to notice the cold reception, while filing it for future reference. "The great mountaineer! . . . Annapurna, nineteen sixty-nine, Nanga Parbat in 'seventy . . .'" The sling had been drawn, now the shot. "*Everest* in 'seventy-two . . . What an honor for a common man like me!"

Nick looked at Simonian's girth. "We need extra rope."

It was like a handshake with a short-circuit, but Simonian's smile was lockjaw. Papazian returned with more cargo.

"My cousin," Simonian said by way of introduction. "Aram Papazian. He has his own boatyard . . . a *very* important man."

Papazian extended a dried leaf of a hand, but Simonian shouted something imperious at him in Armenian, and Papazian continued to load. Nick watched him, checking to see if all the gear they would need had been secured and whether the quality was right, but he continually glanced around with an air of suspicion.

"This car you bring to Ararat?" Simonian was saying to Tony. "It is too bright, too showy. We must change it for a jeep."

"The first place you'd look for climbers is in a jeep," Tony replied. "The last place . . . in a Rolls."

Simonian seemed hardly convinced, but after a show of thinking it over, he slapped his palm on the hood of the car in approval.

"Of course! A beautiful automobile!"

Tony lifted Simonian's hand by his sleeve. "Fingerprints, Simonian. That's how people end up in jail."

The Armenian looked at him oddly, then polished the spot with his dangling shirttail. Nick stared at him: A shark, he thought, a man-eating shark.

Dobbs looked like a coconut asleep on Tahir's lap. The flight in the two-engine Beechcraft, owned by the Ministry of Interior, was tranquilizing, and the separation trauma he had been forced to suffer among all those killer-brutes in the police kennel was gone from his dog brain. At 8000 feet, Tahir, too, breathing pollen-free air, was placid, and Hikmet had not drawn a Kleenex for nearly an hour; he was dozing. The inspector, for whom there was no evidence that he had ever slept, leafed through Simonian's file.

"Simonian was in Nicosia less than two weeks ago," he said, jolting his aide from his winks, Hikmet reaching instinctively for the box with the oval slit. "Perhaps he is already negotiating the sale of the ark to the Metropolitan Museum of New York."

He laughed three times and was about to sneeze, but he checked it. He turned to Hikmet, and reading his thoughts, nodded.

"Ankara? They are getting suspicious. They want to know what business the Istanbul police has in the eastern provinces ... I will have to tell them sooner or later."

Hikmet began to stammer. Tahir stopped him with his old traffic-cop palm.

"Yes ... Later."

Past Ankara, the Rolls-Royce climbed, and when it went through the gates of the Taurus range, the world ended. Anatolian Turkey was a beggar reaching out to an empty horizon. It seemed as inconceivable as it was inevitable that the great mountain would rise on this sweltering endless expanse; for now, it was a journey to nowhere on a sea that had turned to stone, and the air-conditioned Silver Shadow made it all seem like a dream. Yet the presence of the mountain could be felt in their blood, as the moon pulls the tides even on a starless night.

Simonian was in the back seat staring out of the closed window. Tony drove, both hands fighting the wheel, which translated the language of the gutted road into four-letter rattles and knocks. Nick, beside him, had unfolded a rough drawing of Mount Ararat that had been marked with some of the features of interest: the military zone and missile base in the shadow of the north face; an isolated Kurdish settlement at the 6000-foot level; the summer snow line at 14,000 feet; and the mysterious swell Skywatch–2 had found in the Great Ararat ice cap above it.

"The snow line," Tony said pointing at the drawing, "is expected to be at its highest in years, four days from now, on July seventeenth." His eyes, pinned to the orange ribbon of road, narrowed. "Funny, isn't it? ... 'in the seventh month, on the seventeenth day of the month ... That was the day the ark landed on Ararat."

Simonian said piously, "If it is discovered on the seventeenth, by us, of course, that will be a sign from the heavens."

Nick frowned. "Yeah, that God has a calendar in his office."

Simonian chortled.

"The bulge in the ice will be only a hundred and seventy-five feet over the snow line on the seventeenth," Tony went on. "We reach Ararat tomorrow, leaving us three days. I figure it's an honest three days' work to the snow line. Right, Nick?"

"If you're honest." Nick turned around to Simonian. "You guys are honest, ain't you?"

"And you, Mr. Coronado?"

"I watch my ass."

"An honest man watches his ass. Words of wisdom, Mr. Coronado. Worthy of Gregory of Nirek, the greatest Armenian poet."

"On the seventeenth," Tony said recalling the subject, "we start chopping ice."

"Chopping fast," Nick interjected. "There've been storms in the third week of July for the past twelve years. The snow line drops like a curtain."

Tony was impressed. He knew about this recent meteorological phenomenon. It had caused the Hoffmann expedition to fail, leaving one man stranded and killed, but he had not wanted to frighten his companions, particularly Simonian. "You've been keeping up," he said to Nick.

"I've had some free time, lately ... If the storms are really bad, you can turn to ice in a matter of hours. How's that for a heavenly sign?"

No one answered.

Seven

For hours they had seen only farmers' shanties — cubes of darkness under a screaming sun — scattered haphazardly across the fields like dice thrown from a giant's hand. When at last an old gasoline pump outside what pretended to be a roadside café appeared, they stopped, for there was no sign that the next one would not be another hundred miles away. The feeling of being adrift on a boundless terrain was all illusion. They were captives of a beaten path, their true frontiers defined by the ditches along the road.

They got out, seared by the early afternoon heat. A group of Anatolian Turks, young and old but all male, was gathered in an open shed covered with a corrugated tin roof that turned back the sun's rays in blinding light. In spite of the temperature, they were dressed in drab, heavy tunics and woolen caps, engaged in a fierce activity, pounding fistfuls of cash on a board that seemed to be part of a kind of betting game. They paid no mind to the outsiders, though some who were not part of the game drifted to the Rolls, staring with unfocusing eyes, fighting off flies that were hardier than they.

"Opium farmers!" Simonian growled, spitting for emphasis.

The café was dark and almost empty. No one was eating. A few men were playing cards with a numberless deck of all pictures, and they seemed to make a point of not looking up. At the table, Simonian gave a brief discourse on hygiene and the insidiousness of the indigenous germs, and on his recommendation they ordered fresh fruit and cucumbers, tomatoes, and onions, which they washed themselves with bottled water. Simonian ate without utensils, using his pocket knife, and besides the food, he risked only the plates and the salt. Far from offending anyone, they all seemed to gain a measure of respect, but the general attitude remained one of indifference.

A woman, who had been sitting alone in a corner, began an attempt to entertain them. She unveiled a punctured tambourine and a naked belly that rippled like a mound of aspic even before she went into her dance. She was surprisingly young, though her skin, which looked like a sheet of damp cardboard that had been bent around her bones, had been destroyed by the sun, and while she might have passed for under forty, she was probably still in her teens. She moved like a wind-up toy fashioned by a macabre twist of mind; her belly had been given a capacity for numerous articulations, and that was not without hypnotic effect, but it was divided in two unequal humps by a raggedy cleft of scar tissue through which at least one human being, dead or alive, had entered this world.

Simonian ate abundantly. Tony began to study his notebook. He had found a copy of *Black Writing* in the Cinili Kusku Library, a nineteenth-century German translation, and he had copied out several sections. Though his German was barely adequate, he had seen that the *Mashaf Rash* was little more than a prayer book and he had simply transcribed a few passages, but now in rereading them, he found the prayers themselves darkly suggestive of danger, and he wished he had taken down more.

Only Nick gave the dancing girl the light of his eye, allowing her out of good manners alone to let the springs run down, and when the "show" was mercifully over, he handed her a ten-pound note. She took the money and smiled with a pasty mouth that made a cobweb and there was a proposal on her fingertips inviting him somewhere he could not imagine. He ignored her. She showed no trace of disappointment and slunk into her corner. He pushed his plate aside.

He looked at Tony, grating under his apparently intense absorption in his papers, though he had no idea or care what they contained. How could anyone be so immersed in *anything* while sharing the same fetid air the belly dancer breathed? His eyes moved to her. She was drawing the smoke of the smoldering unripe poppy sap through a hookah, which he guessed she had just purchased with the funds he had provided ... They had turned on with laudanum that night before they left for Katmandu. You could buy *anything* in Bombay and you didn't even have to leave your room. They had ridden on clouds and had slid down rainbows in the old wing of the Taj Mahal Hotel, listening to a midnight raga that endured at least two hours, making love that had seemed everlasting. Her belly was smooth.

He was growing more and more uneasy. "So they found some old wood," he shot at Tony with scorn. "That only means there was some old wood up there."

Tony had been reading about the serpent people's belief in metempsychosis. He knew of several religions that accepted the doctrine that the soul after death may pass into the body of an animal, but none, until now, that had established rites for the transmigration to occur during life. But he said nothing of this to Nick, replying to him defensively, feeling irritation.

"And if we find the ark? You don't seem to realize what it would mean." *The* ark? He was astonished at his response. He had never considered what in fact it would mean. His very nature prohibited him from supposing that anything found might be Noah's. *An* ark, perhaps; *something* was on the mountain. The satellite photos were proof enough. But that lone fact demanded, particularly of him, that it could be *anything* — even a Coke bottle and a can of paint, and as Nick, who he realized was being more scientific than he, had just said, some old wood.

"Sure I know what it means," Nick went on. "All that wood, we could open a toothpick factory."

Simonian laughed. Tony threw up his hands and waved for the check, glad that he had been given a chance to show some disdain.

"You want to know what's up there, kid?" Nick said turning on him agitatedly. "I'll tell you what's up there. The same thing that's on top of every mountain. When you get around fifteen thousand feet, there's nothing much to breathe. You're fucking cold and your blood is turning to slush. Your head floats. You can't think human anymore, only about sleep. But you know sleep is death. So you think about death. Then, it hits. You ... or someone else."

"Okay, okay," Tony said. "No one knows better than Nick Coronado. And if I were you, I'd feel the same way. But try to imagine what the discovery of Noah's ark would mean in a world where *nobody* thinks human anymore." To himself, he sounded like the crackpots, but he was being driven. "If you didn't have any religion, or if you had it but wasn't living it, you'd have to start thinking twice, because suddenly there's something real to believe in. A proof. Not a cross made by a machine, or airy words spouted by a priest. Something you can touch with your own hands, Nick."

"Yeah, and if I was you, I'd think like *you*. Shoving my higher morality down everyone's throat. And anybody who didn't like it, well, he'd just never get invited to my swimming pool!"

Nick reddened, getting up to leave. Tony watched him silently. Simonian stared at both of them as one might keep an eye on trouble.

"And besides," Nick said, heading for the door, "there's no ark!"

Somehow, Tony knew then that there was.

When he stepped outside, Nick saw what the betting had been all about, and he felt steam in his veins. Two ferocious dogs, who had been tied down in the maddening sun, were being thrown into a ring, and began at once to tear at one another's flesh, as the Turks stood around them under the open shed roaring for the kill. He stood rigidly, his jaw pumping.

Tony and Simonian came out of the café, and when Tony made a move to steer Nick to the car, he shook him away rudely.

"I wanna watch," Nick snapped. "I like dogs!"

He walked up, as if to get a closer look at the fight, but then he suddenly grabbed one of the bettors by his tunic, lifted him from the ground, and threw him into the ring. The man scrambled to his feet and ran from the dogs, who seemed ready to call a truce and attack him. Disrupted, they began now to growl at the spectators, slamming their bodies against the makeshift wall of cinder blocks that formed the ring. They were unable to leap over the barrier, but the contest was definitely aborted, and the bettors were incensed. One of them drew a knife, and they turned as a mob against Nick.

Nick planted his feet in the ground. He held his arms away from his sides loosely, ready to launch his fists. The men and boys who had been loitering around the Rolls moved in from the rear, forming a knot around the three outsiders.

Tony tried to placate them. He made a guzzling gesture with his thumb. "My friend, he had too much to drink," he said. But they tightened the circle around them. He turned to Simonian. "Tell them, damnit! Say something!"

"Tell 'em we're from the ASPCA!" Nick shouted.

"You crazy bastard!" Tony cried at him hoarsely, as the man with the knife advanced at the head of the others. "You're going to get us killed!"

Nick smiled, pointing with his head toward the road. "I wouldn't let anything happen to you, kid."

Tony saw what Nick had been indicating: a khaki-colored van, preceded by a jeep flying the Turkish and police flags. It approached them, scattering the crowd. They began to fold up their illegal gambling paraphernalia like sidewalk salesmen, while the police watched with boredom.

Tony flared at Nick. "Okay, dog's best friend. That was pretty dumb!"

"I had too much to drink, remember?"

Simonian led the way to the car, but as they opened the doors, an officer called to them from the jeep.

"Please. One moment."

Tony went up to him, leaving the others at the Rolls.

"I am Lieutenant Hazam Hakki. You have been given trouble?" He was a young man, frail, with a thin mustache, and he spoke in a tone of respect that seemed conditioned by the presence of the Rolls.

"Nothing, lieutenant," Tony said trying to sound as important as he possibly could. "We were just leaving." Tony took a step in retreat, but the officer got out of the jeep.

"Please. In which direction are you going?"

"East . . . uh, southeast, to the Caspian. I'm an archaeologist and we're headed for the Belt Cave." He reached into his pocket for his University of Chicago identity card, and when the officer stopped him with a gesture of trust, he felt proud of his fast thinking.

"There is no need to explain. It is I who should like to. We are investigating a kidnapping. A foreigner, reported missing in Istanbul and seen, possibly, in this very area. He is an archaeologist, too." He looked at a scrap of paper taken from his shirt pocket. "Hoffmann . . . Dr. Gregorovius Hoffmann. Do you know him?"

They were everywhere. Tony shook no.

"Very well. Please. I do not wish to delay your journey. It is a long way to the Caspian Sea."

Tony was about to shake Lieutenant Hakki's hand, but Simonian came up and began to speak to him in Turkish. He sounded unctuously courteous, but Hakki began to register a wary look, and he turned back to Tony.

"You said you were going to the Belt Cave. He says you are going to Ararat, to his home. I do not understand."

Tony bit down hard. "Well, you see, we're stopping there first. As you said, it's a long way."

"Yes. It is. You will open the boot of your motor car, please."

The lieutenant went to the trunk, the contents of which would of course suggest if not completely reveal their true intentions. Nick, leaning against it with folded arms, saw Tony's crestfallen face, and understood what was about to ensue. He felt wise at having insisted that his climber's fee be paid in advance, and though he had a desire to provide the services for which he had contracted, he was just as willing to turn back now.

Simonian appeared more distressed than either of them. He raced through the Turkish language, trying to persuade the young lieutenant that there was nothing of interest inside, and shielding him from the eyes of his fellow policemen, he tried to pass him a handful of bills. Hakki brushed the offer aside with a philosophical smile. He was clearly as determined as he was untouchable, and it took a horn blast from the van to interrupt him. Hearing it, he retraced his steps, went around to the back of the truck, stepping inside for a moment or two. When he returned, he waved the Rolls-Royce on.

Tony gunned the engine and flew. After a while, Simonian concocted an elaborate "explanation" for the lieutenant's sudden turnabout, according to which he had purposely bribed him, "knowing all along" that he was being watched by a superior officer; Hakki had been called by the horn to undergo a search, and having passed the test, he lost interest in the affair, since the attention span of a Turk was about "as long as a drunken sparrow's."

Neither of them credited a word of what Simonian said, and they remained hopelessly unenlightened, but Nick could not rid himself of a haunting feeling that he had heard Dobbs's Sicilian bark emerge from the van.

Eight

"**K**urds! A terrible people!"

The windows of the Rolls were safely closed, allowing Simonian to cry out with seismic contempt at the band of nomads leading their flocks across the burned earth. But they seemed to feel the shockwaves of his bile nonetheless. They stared back with eyes that looked out of their goathair robes like stones lying in a fire.

The car swept past them, unavoidably blowing dust in their faces, and Simonian rattled on. "We have a saying: 'When you speak to a Kurd, hands in your pockets, your shoes strapped tight, and your back to a friend.' But it is better to carry a gun."

"Simonian is our ethnologist," Tony remarked to Nick.

"Some of my best friends are ethnologists," Nick said.

Tony smiled and turned around to catch Simonian's reaction, which was one of incomprehension with malice thrown in for good measure.

Nick, watching the road, suddenly shouted a warning. Tony looked ahead, slamming the brakes, skidding, and veering to a halt. A dead horse, covered with an undulating layer of red ants, lay across the road, blocking it completely.

A leathery-skinned man in peasant clothing came up to the car slowly, humbly. He smiled. His teeth looked like chips of charcoal. Tony lowered the electric window, and the man, clasping his hands, began to plead with him in Kurdish.

"He says he was on his way to the hospital in Kars," Simonian translated. "Some nonsense about his daughter. It is some kind of Kurdish trick. There may be others."

Nick and Tony looked around. The Kurd's daughter sat beside a rock about twenty feet from the roadside, her body and head covered in black, roughly woven woolens, her arm swathed in a burlap bandage. She turned her face toward the men, lowering her eyes. She could not have been more than twenty years old. Her skin was the color of bittersweet chocolate, and as smooth as the same substance when melted. She had obviously been spared the pastoral labors that made even children look withered and old, and she had a countenance that seemed almost aristocratic.

Simonian questioned the man with a poker in his voice, and the Kurd began again to beseech them.

"He says there is a bus in the morning. It passes on the Aghri road. He is asking for a ride. Better to give him some coins and be on our way."

Tony glanced again at the girl. He caught her eyes darting around a corner of sunlight to hide. "Tell him we'll take him."

Nick said nothing, but his face showed outright disapproval. Simonian erupted.

"But you are foolish, Tony! We will lose six hours. If we are lucky. You do not know these people. He will rob —"

Tony reached back and opened the rear door, motioning for the Kurd to get inside. The man smiled broadly and ran to get his daughter.

"Say something, Coronado!" Simonian implored. "It is madness to get involved!"

"I think you're both nuts. But it's his car."

The two Kurds slid into the back of the Rolls. Simonian blackened and shriveled like a burning matchstick in his effort to stay as far from them as possible. The young woman, holding her bandaged arm, smiled to all of them thankfully, graciously.

The Rolls turned for the Aghri road to Kars, and when it had disappeared and the dust had returned to the ground, four hooded men came out from the behind the boulders. They removed the dead horse from the road. A fifth man stood in the distance and watched. He had a face like the bark of an oak, and around his neck he wore a serpent made of gold. The others called him "Shaikh."

It was dark when they arrived at the Aghri junction, and they camped in a wood of poplars, sharing their fire and the light of a moon that was rising with the man and his daughter.

They had been silent, troubleless traveling companions, talking only when questioned, and the girl spoke but once giving her name. The Kurd's name was Yussef. Hers was Sippara, and that had struck a memory chord for Tony. He knew the history of Chaldea, and he remembered Sippara as the City of the Sun, where "the beginning, the middle, and the end" of all recorded knowledge had been buried before the Flood, but he knew of no link between the Assyro-Babylonian cultures and the Kurdish. He had watched her in the rearview mirror. She looked oddly serene, though she seemed to be favoring a pain in her arm, biting her lips whenever the car hit a bump. Slowing, he had tried to avoid the worst of the road, and they had paid for that in time and Simonian's implacable mood.

Now Simonian tended the fire, and Sippara sat close to the flames, for the nighttime temperature had plunged. Tony, a blanket thrown over his shoulders, was bent under the open hood of the Rolls, checking the level of engine oil, and Nick, wearing his 60/40 parka, poured gasoline, filling the hundred-liter tank. When Tony went around to the trunk for a can of oil, he noticed Sippara. She seemed to be trembling as she leaned toward the fingers of the fire. He took a blanket from the back of the car and went to her.

Nick had observed Tony's interest in the young woman, though it could only be seen in the subtle movements of his eyes. Amateur, he thought, fucking amateur. He had climbed with amateurs before, and it had always brought trouble, sometimes death. Amateurs broke the rules, and the rule of rules was to permit not the slightest distraction. Every step was, had to be, a foothold. On whatever you placed your toe had to be attached to the center of the earth, and knowing that it was, was a full-time job. But amateurs dreamed; they dreamed of nibbling on the magic candy that would sweeten the empty stomach of existence, and as dreams are the false prophets of the dreamer, amateurs were easily led astray. Monique had been an amateur

He looked over at Tony. The blanket was draped around Sippara, and she had allowed him to unravel her bandage to redress her wound. She's probably got the clap, too, he thought, and he'd be peeing blood in the snow on the mountain if her old man wasn't around — if he *was* her old man. And where was the old man, anyway?

He heard a stir behind the car and looked up. Nothing. Then a rustling sound. He walked around to the open back door and caught sight of the Kurd running deeper into the woods. He saw the rifle holster on the ground. Empty. The Kurd had vanished into the night. Nick moved slowly in the space through which he had gone.

Her forearm was badly infected, bloated and logged with pus. He could see the teeth marks of an animal bite, and bluish red lightninglike streaks radiating to her wrist and her elbow: the not-so-early signs of gangrene, which he had learned to recognize on a summer dig in the lower Euphrates. She needed drainage, antibiotics, antitetanus, and the whole painful series of treatments to combat rabies, and he knew she needed them now, not tomorrow in Kars, where by the time she would arrive at the hospital — whatever that might be like — they would probably act first with a saw.

He went to the car for the medical kit. At least he could give her penicillin and the antitetanus shots and clean and rebandage the wound with antiseptic materials. He tried to find Nick but he saw that Sippara and he were completely alone. He knew where Simonian had gone, since he had announced that he had to attend to matters of a private nature, but he wondered about the others, concluding that they too had been similarly called. He shrugged and returned to Sippara.

She smiled when she saw the medicines and offered her arm without reticence, as if as a token of trust.

"Was it a dog?" he asked as he filled the syringe.

She shook her head, not to say no, but that she did not understand. He pointed to the wound questioningly and arf-arfed. She laughed, again shaking no, this time with comprehension.

Then she picked up a twig and made a sign that she would draw the offending beast on the ground. He told her to wait and he injected both drugs below her shoulder, staring for a moment at the velour smoothness of her skin. He gave her the emptied labeled vials with a word-and-gesture explanation that she show them to the hospital doctors. She seemed to understand.

She had reacted to the pinch of the hypodermics only with appreciative sighs, and now she all but cooed as he washed the ugly bite with alcohol and began to bind her arm in gauze, while with her free hand she scratched a figure in the soil.

She made an ogrelike creature that stood upright, though not entirely erect. It looked like a gorilla, which was a geographical impossibility. A monkey, perhaps. He added a tail to the drawing. She giggled, shaking her head, and rubbing it out.

"Keh . . . li," she said slowly as if that would help him understand.

A bear on its hindlegs? A long tail on a bear would be laughable. "Bear?" he replied, trying to imagine how he might imitate one.

"Kehli." Or something that sounded as if it were spelled that way.

He studied the teeth marks. He had of course been trained to identify animals by teeth remains, even fragments of dental sockets and jawbones, but he knew of none that had a form quite like that which showed on her arm, though it had become distorted by the swelling. He could see the unmistakable impressions of the canines, but they were no deeper than the others, as they would have been from a bear bite. From the space between the two canines and the position of the incisors and molars, he could gauge the size and shape of the jaw, and when it struck him that it seemed remarkably reminiscent of a human's, he drew back from the thought, and returned to the idea of a bear. They were nowhere near bear country, but he knew that Eurasian bears inhabited Mount Ararat near the snow line and it seemed likely that the same species could be found throughout the Anatolian ranges. As he was unfamiliar with their dentition, he settled for that theory, and he could not help but wonder if she had come from Ararat.

He asked her, stretching his words for simplicity and inventing a sign language as he went along. He could see that she understood that he was inquiring as to where she was from, but the word "Ararat" apparently meant nothing to her.

"*Aghri Dagh?*" he said, using the Turkish name.

"*Ne.*"

He knew that was a negative, but it was clear that she still had not understood. He tried the Armenian equivalent. "*Masis?*" Nothing. What was it the Persians called it? "*Koh-i-Nouh?*" Her eyes lit, but he knew he was only part of the way there, and he had run out of synonyms.

He took the twig from her hand. He drew a mountain with two peaks, one the big brother of the other. She was enjoying the game immensely, and now she nodded. They were communicating, but had she recognized the mountain as Ararat? He sketched the outline of a boat on the higher peak. She nodded again.

"*Nouh,*" she said, lowering her head as if she had uttered the name of God.

"Noah?"

"*Nouh.*" Her head said yes with excitement. She made a circle around the mountain with her finger and pointed to her chest.

She had come from Ararat. They both smiled. There was a moment of triumph, and another of silent celebration, then an urge to continue that was as warm as the glow from the fire.

He began to climb the mountain with his fingers, and he pointed to where Nick had been standing, then he made caricature strokes with his hands and his face miming Simonian's hulk and surly expression. She laughed loudly, saying what had to be yes, yes, yes in Kurdish. They were playing well now, speaking body Esperanto, even gossiping, and she seemed as delighted as he. Now his fingers climbed the mountain once more. Then Nick, and his fingers again. Then fat, pouting Simonian — which made her giggle — and fingers. He knew he should not be gabbing this way about their plans to someone from so near the mountain, but she was going to the hospital, and they would have been to Ararat and back by the time she returned. In any event she failed to understand. Her face wrinkled in an exaggerated, quizzical look. Don't you get it? he asked in their private language. Me, Nick, and funny old Simonian, we're climbing Ararat, or whatever you call it, to get to the ark . . . to *Nouh*. Get it?

She got it. Like a spike impaling her soul. Like treachery pie in the face. She shrank from him, tearing his blanket from her shoulders.

"*Ne!*" she cried, shaking her head in utter disbelief, and when he failed to retreat, to pardon his outrage with a thousand pleas for forgiveness, she slumped, murmuring, "*Ne, ne, ne . . .*"

Tony stared at her; they were no longer in communion.

Gunfire hammered on the nighttime air, two shots in rapid succession. Sippara looked up in a fright, and Tony spun around to the sound. Simonian came running from the woods, closing the belt around his waist.

"What was it?" he asked breathlessly. "Where is Coronado?"

" I don't know."

The Kurd appeared in a shaft of moonlight. Tony's rifle was silhouetted in one hand and something dangled from the other, clutched in his fist. He held it up against the lunar disk: two dead mountain hares — a proud dinner offering to his hosts.

"Sonofabitch can really shoot," Nick said, coming up between Tony and Simonian.

The Kurd walked toward the fire, grinning expansively, but when he saw Sippara sitting on the ground, looking profoundly disturbed, he handed the slain animals to Tony and dropped to her side. He began to question her, more and more insistently as she failed to respond.

Simonian motioned silently to Nick and Tony that the Kurd still held the weapon, but no one moved. The Kurd saw Tony's Ararat on the ground, and he shouted harsh demands at his daughter. She nodded and wept.

Nick and Tony turned to Simonian, who had a look of impending emergency that was adrenalizing his stance. The Kurd, still in possession of the rifle, walked up to Tony with icy indignation, and though he carried the rifle in a harmless position, he seemed to be trying to contain a murderous impulse. Simonian stabbed at him with a swipe of his hand, attempting to seize the Kalashnikov, but the Kurd reacted simultaneously, spinning it to the ready and thrusting it forward at Simonian's barrel chest.

Simonian stepped back. The Kurd slowly lifted his eyes from Simonian and revolved to Tony. He threw the rifle to Tony's feet, and he took his sobbing daughter by her hand. They turned and went for the road.

Nick and Tony watched them fade into the darkness. Simonian suddenly dove for the rifle, but Tony was quicker, bringing the heel of his boot down on Simonian's hand. He cried out in pain, his fingers crushed around the trigger. Tony eased the pressure barely enough for Simonian to slide his hand free, and he picked up the rifle himself.

"What in fuck's name was that all about?" Nick asked them both.

"They don't like the way I draw," said Tony, though Nick was hardly satisfied with that answer and showed it.

"They are superstitious about Ararat," Simonian said nursing his hand. "They are fanatics and savages, and Tony insulted their god." He glared at Tony.

"We were having a friendly chat in sign language," Tony said to Nick, avoiding detail. "I guess she read me wrong."

Nick said nothing.

"You are foolish, Tony, to have stopped me," Simonian went on. "The Kurds are like wolves in the forest. They must be tamed by fire."

Nick picked up the dead hares. He hung them by their hind legs from a low branch. He made thin, circular incisions just above their rear feet with a hunting knife. He drew back the skin, and in a single motion, as if he were removing a pullover sweater, he stripped each of them to the flesh almost bloodlessly.

"Amateurs!" he muttered.

Nine

They followed the Aras River, racing the rapids to the east, heading for the Plain of Igdir and the north face of the mountain. They were in the old kingdom of Armenia now, stirring the same volcanic dust that had covered the footprints of Marco Polo's return.

The sun had awakened this dawn full of morning resolutions to whip their air-conditioner at its own game. It hurled its heat in giant boulders, and it gilded every color, including those of the grasses, the fields of lava, and even the haze in the sky.

The experience of the night before remained undiscussed but it gnawed like too much to drink hung over. Nick and Tony were silent, their eyes pointing at the distance, waiting for the mountain to chin itself over the horizon, and as they moved closer to Ararat, Simonian began to puff out like a rooster, crowing with national pride.

"The Aras can flow for a thousand years more," he said bitterly, "and it will not wash away the Armenian blood that has been spilled in its waters, on this side of the river at the hands of the Kurds, but mostly the Turks, where even the Great Assassin Abdul-Hamid was outdone by the genocide of nineteen fifteen and 'sixteen. In Turkey, they slaughtered our mothers and fathers, our brothers and sisters, but on the other side of the river, in *Soviet* Armenia, they slaughtered our freedom."

"Lucky for us they never got you, Simonian," Nick said, knowing crocodile tears when he saw them.

Simonian chuckled. "Hakob Meliq Simonian is ungettable, Coronado."

He had been waiting for this moment. "Tahir doesn't seem to think so."

Simonian recoiled. "You know this man?"

"He's got a brother in Connekticut."

"He is a fool! And Ankara knows it. During the war I helped the Americans. I was with the freedom fighters against Stalin. And this pig of a man accused me of being a spy for the Russians. Against my *own* people! Imagine that!"

"Imagine that," Nick said.

"Of course, the charges were dropped."

"Of course."

Simonian sneered at the back of Nick's head. Tony saw it in the mirror. Nick felt it.

"There is a turn toward the river up ahead," Simonian said leaning forward. "It is not more than five hundred meters. We are home."

Before them lay bleached, ashy terrain with a stubble of yellow grass. Stunted eucalyptus rose along the banks of the Aras. The mountain could still not be glimpsed. The horizon was blocked by huge formations of lava, and when they took Simonian's road, it was lost again behind trees. It was near, however, tantalizingly near, and they had only to climb a knoll to see the entire massif. They had already passed the outlying flats of Nakhitchevan, which in Armenian means "Noah's home," where the Patriarch planted the first vineyard after the Flood and fell naked in a drunken sleep when he drank the new wine. But they had seen no vines.

On Simonian's instructions, they stopped in a clearing, where four dilapidated Volkswagen buses were parked, their tires removed, their wheels up on lava blocks. There were six or seven children at play among an equal number of chickens. A peasant woman came out of one of the VWs, and seeing the men emerge from the Rolls, shouted a stout greeting. Another woman appeared, and before long still three more stepped out of the buses, all of them standing in full-dress smiles for the new arrivals.

Simonian greeted them all with bear hugs and kisses, as the children tugged on his trousers. All five women looked as solid as tree trunks, and the sum total of their ages could not have been much more than a hundred years, though their cumulative weight was certainly close to half a ton. They had a common sensuality around the mouth, a kind of longing that seemed within reach of being in some manner soon fulfilled. Nick and Tony watched the homecoming patiently.

"What do you say to a Volkswagen harem?" Tony asked Nick.

"Why don't you ask 'em how many miles they get to the gallon."

Simonian introduced his women, and they did a sort of curtsy one by one. "Ah," he sighed when their names had been exhausted, "it's not an easy task for an old one like me to be the provider for five healthy women . . . Armenian women!"

He smiled wide enough to cover all of them with his happiness and they grinned elatedly in return, after which he began to bark gruffly in Armenian and they, the children, and the chickens, too, quickly disappeared. He turned to his companions, now, smiling again, and motioned to them to follow as he led them around the buses under a natural bridge spanning rockface to a clearing.

"Welcome to Ararat!" he suddenly cried. "Mother of the World!" His arm swept upward grandiosely offering them an unobstructed view of the mountain, as if it were his.

The sun had burned off the morning haze. It stood at the zenith, and there was no cloud in the sky whose shoulders could intrude on the panorama. Ararat ascended from the plain the way the gods had come down from the heavens, in an aura of mystical light, careening from the silvery edges of basalt and ice with an intensity the eye could not very long endure. Though not by a far cry the tallest mountain in the world, it stood higher than Everest above its surrounding plateau, lifting out of the folds of its foothills as if it were being drawn from its moorings by the call of infinite space. At this time of year, only Great Ararat, its nobler, more majestic peak, wore a mantle of snow — the ermine robe of kingship. A wind stirred on the plain, filling their eyes with sand. It whispered around their ears, daring them to approach the mountain, and laughing as it rushed by at the puny figures they cut in its shadow.

"They say the stars are visible at noon from the top of the Mother of the World," Simonian vaunted.

"I'll settle for the sun," said Nick, thinking of the storms.

Tony said nothing. He had heard nothing, except the mocking wind.

In the late afternoon, when the light was beginning to fade, they drove the Rolls closer to the mountain, following a back road that wound between rocks. Simonian had selected a cave where they could hide the car until their return from the climb, and after they had rolled it inside, they began to camouflage the opening, making a curtain of foliage.

The cave was at a dead end off the road, beside a barbed, double chain-link fence, beyond which lay the Ararat missile base. There were signs posted every few yards warning in Turkish and English, "Trespassers and/or loiterers will be placed under immediate arrest; photograph equipment will be confiscated," though it was difficult to imagine what anyone might want to photograph from where they stood. They could see only a series of watchtowers along the fence, which isolated an enormous area around the north curve of the mountain, and in the distance lay several low concrete buildings of nondescript design.

"For once, the Turks are respecting our beliefs," Simonian said pointing to the fence. He smiled, waiting for Nick's and Tony's attention, and then went on. "It is against God's will for an Armenian to cast his eyes on the ark. Noah is our oldest ancestor and we are the children of Japheth, his son, and therefore the first people after the Flood." He gestured again toward the fence. "So, we were right to call Ararat the forbidden mountain." Now he grinned. "But I, Hakob Meliq Simonian, will show you the way."

Nick smirked.

They looked across the flatland. In the oblique, fading light they could see a long swath running straight through the grass, a wide stripe made evident by grass that was paler and shorter than the growth on either side. Tony recognized it as the sign of some sort of once-existing road. It seemed a road to nowhere, and when he remarked as much, Simonian corrected him, explaining that it had been a secret airfield during the Second World War.

"I built it," he said, revolving his calloused hands, as if he were polishing doorknobs. "I told you I was with the freedom fighters, but it was on this side that I worked. When the Turks finally declared war against Germany, American agents came here. To help the Armenians. A very important mission. Very secret. I was their contact man. The Russians were worried about their borders. And why not? The Armenians want to be free. Stalin sent in his spies. They killed the Americans." He looked at Nick. "I know you will say something 'humorous' now, about how I managed to survive. Let me save you the trouble. True, I was unimportant. But I was awarded a medal."

Nick raised his eyebrows in a gesture of "respect." "Oh," he said, "from which side?"

Simonian gave a roundhouse laugh, which ended abruptly when he saw that Tony had opened the trunk of the Rolls and had removed his rifle, and as he slung it over his shoulder, Simonian stopped him.

"That you must leave behind."

"Like hell I will."

"We are safer without it. One shot on the mountain can be heard for miles. But there is a greater danger. Listen." He turned to Ararat and called out in a thunderous voice, "*Masis!*"

The sound pushed across the valley, striking the side of the mountain, which returned a tremulous echo of its Armenian name that was followed by the roar of falling rock.

"You can have an avalanche to order. Just shout when you want one." Simonian turned to Nick. "The stones of Ararat are very loose."

Tony looked at Nick, who nodded in agreement with Simonian. Not that he trusted anything Simonian said, particularly what he announced as his motives. But there was no doubt about the threat of rockslides, and he felt that if no one were armed, it would be he himself who in almost any circumstance would hold the advantage.

"Like the man said," he replied to Tony's querying eyes, "we're safer without it."

Tony had reasons of his own for not wanting to part with the Kalashnikov, not the least of which was that familiar, undefinable feeling that others had called his "divining rod." It was his finding-sense, and it had been strengthening with every step closer to the mountain. By now it whined steadily like a struck tuning fork. As always, it gave no clue as to what he would find, but when he did, it told him, he would need a gun.

But he saw no way, now that he had been "outvoted" by Nick and Simonian, how he could insist on remaining armed. He looked at the mountain. The sun had settled behind it a while ago, and only the peaks stood between the end of daylight and the beginning of night. He repeated Simonian's cry, and he heard the echo and the tumbling rocks.

"A destroying eminence," he mused as he returned the rifle to the car.

"A rockpile," Nick grunted, locking the steel shaft of a 500-millimeter ice ax in his mountaineering belt.

The UGA Memorandums—II

(July 1977)

TO: THE PRESIDENT
FROM: THE DEPARTMENT OF STATE/RMS.
RE: UGA

Since our last meeting, I have given as much time to reflection as my duties allow regarding your most enlightening interpretations of your readings of those chapters of the Good Book, which, as fate would have it, concern us at this time. I was particularly impressed by your theory that the episode concerning Noah's rush to plant a vineyard and culminating in his drunkenness does not accord with the picture of him rendered earlier as a wholly righteous man, the Lord's choice to survive the Flood, and that it probably represents a late insertion into the Scriptures by a scurrilous author with mercantile interests (i.e., to promote the consumption of wine and wine products). How much like our own times! And how right you are that — should the Ark be found — you must guard against maneuvers by lobbyists of any kind to commercialize such a glorious and solemn occasion.

On the other hand, your program for public information, prepared by the Presidential Press Secretary — from your first appearance on worldwide television to announce the historic, awesome event, on through the minting of commemorative stamps for issuance on July 17, 1978, is bound to bring unprecedented praise for your Administration and win the hearts of the American people regardless of race, color, or creed.

HANDWRITTEN NOTE BY THE PRESIDENT: To RMS: Let's not forget the numismatics — how about a commemorative coin: a half-dollar piece in a plastic, see-through case, with my profile (on the heads), and Noah, staff in hand, riding shotgun against the Flood (on the tails). I see him standing on the prow of the Ark, his long white beard and flowing hair whipping in the wind and the rain. He should look a little like Charlton Heston, but not too much. What do you think?

TO: THE PRESIDENT
FROM: THE DIRECTOR, CENTRAL INTELLIGENCE AGENCY
SUBJECT: UGA/OPERATION ICEPICK

As requested, this Agency's Coordinative Analysis Division

(CAD) has conducted an interdisciplinary study of *all available intelligence* with the cooperation of the Historical Analysis Division (HAD) and the Special Office of Strategic Operations (SOSO). The following is a summary of the Joint CAD/HAD/SOSO Report:

There exists a gap in our knowledge of the zone under scrutiny as compared with that of the Russians, who have long manifested a curious interest in Mount Ararat. Indeed, the first recorded conquest of the 16,945-foot peak was made by an alpinist in the Russian Imperial Service, J. J. von Parrot, who with two Russian soldiers and three Armenians reached the summit in September 1829, scaling the southeast face.

Since then there have been a substantial number of expeditions, only some of them successful, including several made by Americans, though few in recent years due to the Turkish ban.

What characterizes the Russian ventures, both in the pre-Revolutionary and Soviet eras, as uniquely different from ours and all others, may be seen in their scope and intent. While the non-Russian explorations have been centered around finding evidence of the biblical vessel, usually conducted by small groups with theological interests, Moscow has invariably sent its climbers to gather *military or quasi-military intelligence*, and its missions have always been made up of military personnel and scientists, sometimes numbering as many as 150 persons.

It is true that in 1916 a Russian pilot named Roskovitsky, making perhaps the first aerial reconnaissance flight of Great Ararat (which is in itself significant), claimed to have observed "the hulk of a huge ship," jutting out from the glacial ice into a frozen lake, but the "documents" associated with a corroborative expedition to the all but inaccessible north face (undertaken by the army, incidentally) are said to have "disappeared" after the October Revolution.

In the period just prior to the end of World War II, and as late as 1949, however, an undetermined number of ascents were made by mountaineers of the Red Army. A search through the archives of the OSS reveals that United States intelligence reported that these ascents were of a *strategic nature as regards the security of Moscow's southern flank*, thought by Stalin to be extremely vulnerable in Soviet Armenia. These early reports suggest that *strategic weapons may have been installed at the summit,* and when it is recalled that 1949 marks the year in which the Russians exploded their first *nuclear device,* it is not difficult to surmise what the nature of this installation might have been. The same year, moreover, saw the formation of the North Atlantic Treaty Alliance (NATO), and work began on the Turkish military base that lies along the Frontier Defense Perimeter (FDP), which passes between the northern foothills of Mount Ararat and the borders of the Soviet Union.

Although this area has been designated by Ankara as a military zone (TMZ), off-limits to all but the local residents (mostly Kurdish nomads and Turkish Armenians), the restricted region, several times in the 1950s, was reported by this Agency as having been infiltrated by Russian agents, who have from time to time employed persons from the native populace as operatives (notably Turkish Armenians who appear also to have been wartime operatives for our own OSS, but probably double agents for the NKVD, the predecessor agency of the KGB).

With the advent of increasingly sophisticated ballistic missile hardware (IRBMs), and its installation in the TMZ, KGB penetration seems to have been focused on multiple undercover missions (perhaps five or six), guided by the local operatives, which sought to reach the Great Ararat summit for reasons that have never been learned. These clandestine sorties appear to have ended by the late 1950s, although it cannot be excluded that they have not continued all along undetected, or by other unobserved means (e.g., helicopter drops).

Although there exist no hard data that would explain the aims of Soviet activity on Mount Ararat, it should not be difficult to construct *a minimum profile, based on the foregoing intelligence, of Moscow's possible intentions.* It is not within the mandate of this study to undertake such a task; however, it is clear that at least three hypotheses must be considered:

a. the Great Ararat ice cap has been effectively armed with *nuclear devices designed to neutralize the* TMZ FDP.

b. there is a continuity of operations of unknown significance (*see note at the end of this report*) reaching back to tsarist times (e.g., from Col. Khodzko's astronomical-topographical expedition in 1850 — or even Von Parrot's 1829 ascent — to the present day).

c. the Soviets are in possession of intelligence similar to that gathered by Skywatch–2 and are carrying out (or, in view of the apparent cessation of operations prior to 1960, have already carried out to their satisfaction) their own investigations.

It should be emphasized that none of the above propositions is mutually exclusive with regard to the others, i.e., they may all be true, or any one or two of them may be true. The equally valid possibility that *none* of them is true would render Soviet activity on Mount Ararat as being totally irrelevant and would close every door but one: that the origir o UGA is either

i. supernatural (Noah's Ark?); or
ii. extraterrestrial (an extraplanetary spaceship?)

NOTE ON PROPOSITION B: By "unknown significance" we do not wish to convey that we are completely in the dark. Mount Ararat, it should be recalled, is a volcano. It is craterless and has not been active in historic times, but is nonetheless a kind of geological, virtually hollow cap over the vast quantities of energy stored beneath the earth's surface. In fact, the Turkish government has established an experimental geothermal energy station at the foot of the mountain (in the TMZ) as part of a national program to tap underground sources of high-temperature water, which when released as steam can be converted to electricity (such installations already exist in other volcanic countries, e.g., Italy, India, et al.). The military value of this form of energy remains minimal, however. But if a Great Power, such as the Soviet Union, were to learn how to harness not the heated water, but *volcanic energy* itself, this would represent a major breakthrough. It is estimated that the potential energy output contained within the volcanic interstices beneath Mount Ararat is equal to the force of *100,000 one-hundred megaton nuclear warheads*.

No such force has ever been released on this planet. However, it is *not* of doomsday proportions. It *is* powerful enough *to alter the earth's inclination toward the sun* by a fraction of a degree, the principal effect of which would be *a radical shift in global weather patterns,* a redistribution of macroclimates *favoring some countries over others.* Hence there is further reason for concern over early and continued Soviet presence on Mount Ararat.

NOTE BY THE DIRECTOR: I favor proposition A; the DOD leans toward B. I've found no one who agrees with C, and (i) or (ii) is a bit too fanciful for anyone's tastes around here. We now have a resident agent at the site (Franklin Tompkins), who, as per your instructions, remains, however, unbriefed re UGA and Operation Icepick.

HANDWRITTEN NOTE BY THE PRESIDENT: To RMS: There's too much speculation going on at the CIA and DOD. As long as we can keep the Russkies off the mountain, and that shouldn't be too difficult (though we don't want the Turks brought in on this in any way), the Thing up there is contained, and I expect we'll know soon enough what it is. Meantime, let's keep the CIA's fingers out of this pudding. I'm counting on you. By the way, bear in mind that if it does turn out to be Noah's Ark, according to the Bible, Noah comes hundreds of years before Abraham and Moses, so any Israeli claims that he was Jewish, which could be used for political leverage, are to be vehemently discouraged (*tactfully* — don't forget the you-know-whos-in-which-big-cities-at-home). We don't want to find ourselves in a situation where Tel Aviv starts upping the ante for any future internationalization of Jerusalem in exchange for the internationalization of Ararat. But, meantime, mum continues to be the word.

TO: THE PRESIDENT
FROM: THE DIRECTOR, CENTRAL INTELLIGENCE AGENCY
SUBJECT: UGA/OPERATION ICEPICK, URGENT ADDITIONAL INTELLIGENCE

The following are the texts of a telex received at EDT 0400 hours today from Resident Agent Tompkins, Ararat Station, and the Agency's reply EDT 0905 hours:

TILLIE [the Turkish authorities] SCHEDULES TOP-SECRET GEOTHERMAL ENERGY EXPERIMENTAL TEST TWENTIETH JULY SEVENTEEN HUNDRED HOURS STOP TILLIE SCIENTISTS PREDICT TEST SPECTACULAR SUCCESS STOP TILLIE REVVING FOR MAXIMUM INTERNATIONAL PRESS TO BOLSTER ALICE'S [Ankara's] IMAGE AND MAKE OPEC CRINGE AS ALICE TOYS WITH PROMISE OF ENERGY SELF-SUFFICIENCY BY 1983 TO CLOUT CLAMOROUS DOMESTIC OPPOSITION STOP TOMPKINS.

FOR TOMPKINS VIA AZORES CIRCUIT ARARAT STATION TMZ: INCREASE DEBRIEFINGS ON TEST COUNTDOWN STOP POSSIBILITY RHODA [Russian] PRESENCE MONITORING TEST STOP YOUR MISSION PRIORITY UPPED TO FOURTH DEGREE.

As you know, Tompkins is unbriefed re UGA and has therefore not been mandated to assess the dangers posed by the test release of geothermal energy at the site. You can see from our reply to Tompkins that I have ordered that the degree of urgency concerning his assignment be raised. However, I suggest that it be set at the highest priority, and, without really leveling with him, that he be instructed to take immediate soundings regarding the above-mentioned dangers, with a view toward the suspension of the test by Ankara, if necessary, under a cover story, of course. Please advise.

HANDWRITTEN NOTE BY THE PRESIDENT: To RMS: We're in a pickle. I still don't want the CIA in on this all the way. Latest polls show CIA's rep continues to tarnish at home, so it's too risky if anything goes wrong, especially if the Thing turns out to be you-know-what and we ruin it. Yet we don't want the test to melt the ice and have the Thing — whatever it might be — sticking out all over the place, or, God forbid if it is a Russky superbomb, setting it off *ourselves!* I'm not having my Administration go down in history as having pushed the Russkies' red button! Any ideas?

PART TWO

(July 15–18, 1977)

A couple of circles around the snow-capped dome and then a long, swift glide down the side and then we suddenly came upon a perfect little gem of a lake; blue as an emerald [sic], but still frozen over on the shady side. We circled around and returned for another look at it. Suddenly my companion whirled around and yelled something, and excitedly pointed down at the overflow end of the lake. I looked and nearly fainted! A submarine! No, it wasn't . . . We flew down as close as safety permitted and took several circles around it. We were surprised when we got close to it at the immense size of the thing, for it was as long as a city block and would compare very favorably in size to the modern battleships of today.

> Vladimir Roskovitsky,
> *The New Eden* (1940)

CHRISTIAN-HATING COMMUNISTS
DIG UP NOAH'S ARK AND BURN IT!

The Russians are reported to have found Noah's Ark and burned it. According to reliable Moscow sources, the Communists dug the ancient ship out of a glacier high atop Mt. Ararat just across the Russian border in Turkey. Teams of Russian explorers dismantled the ancient ship and took it back to the capital where they burned the pieces. They also are reported to have found about thirty animals frozen aboard the ship in its hold.

> *The National Enquirer* (1974)

Ten

In a soundproof room at the TMZ missile base, Nazim Aziz Tahir was seated with Hikmet, his aide, addressing Colonel Hakim Hakim, of the Turkish Army, and "Major" Franklin Tompkins, a "military attaché" from the United States Embassy at Ankara.

"Simonian," he said loudly, "is the biggest liar in all of Turkey."

The colonel, head of security operations in the TMZ, and the so-called major listened intently to the inspector from Istanbul, although Tompkins, at this late date in his career, could do absolutely nothing to conceal the permanent crease of skepticism that marked the synthetic fabric of his expression.

Tahir blew an invasion from his nose; the enemy in eastern Turkey was a whole new horde thrown into combat by a floral Genghis Khan.

"Gentlemen," Tahir said, standing now, booming his voice at the American (major, indeed, he thought), "he is a smuggler, a dealer in opium and stolen art treasures. But, Major Tompkins, a Russian spy, he is not!"

"We happen to think otherwise, inspector," Tompkins drawled in a Georgia accent he would not have dared to turn quite this loose in Washington. "Listen, there's less room between here and the Russian border than you need to skin a cat without getting a mouthful of hair."

Tahir looked at him quizzically. "Ah, you Americans! You are still living in the nineteen fifties. In the nineteen fifties he was a Russian spy. Now he has — how do you say — moved in with the times."

"What does Istanbul want him for?" Colonel Hakim Hakim asked, seeing Tompkins take a thimbleful of umbrage.

"Lying. Smuggling. Drugs. And stealing Byzantine icons. However, there is no evidence. However, I am a patient man." Tahir began to walk around the room slowly, showing his patience. His watery eyes peered into the past. "In the nineteen fifties, I had him for spying. I would have been made Chief of Police!" He stopped behind Hikmet and put his fatherly hands on the young detective's shoulders. "The rope was around his neck. The trap door was pulled. He was hanging!" Hikmet gasped. Tahir's hands had little by little been interfering with his supply of oxygen. Tahir threw up his arms in despair. "A government amnesty! He has a scar on his neck this thick," he cried bitterly, indicating the size. "The next time, I will make him look at it — without a mirror!"

"Well, I may be as slow as a pond, inspector," Tompkins said, "but the only things worth smuggling or stealing around here, with all due respect to your great country, are military secrets. If that's not his cup of tea, how do you explain his being here?"

Tahir glanced at Hikmet. Military secrets, indeed! he said to him with his eyes. He turned back to Tompkins. "I explain it, sir, with an old Turkish proverb: 'Where there is the smell of rotten fish, there is rotten fish.'"

Tompkins looked at him as if something had been lost in the translation. But Tahir merely smiled, attempting no elaboration.

"What about the other two?" asked Hakim Hakim, who was growing slightly uncomfortable with Tahir's monumental self-containedness and Tompkins's indecipherable idioms.

Tahir shrugged. "An archaeologist and a mountain climber ... Mere children in the hands of Simonian." He nodded at Hikmet, who stood. Tahir, bowing his head politely to the others, prepared to take leave. "If you need any more information," he concluded, his gaze on Tompkins and an open hand aimed at Hikmet, "my assistant will tell you everything!"

They went out, Tahir in his own special way fortifying his mucous membranes for a second wave of the plundering hordes.

"Does he know about the geothermal test?" Tompkins asked Hakim Hakim when they had gone.

"He must. It is difficult to keep secrets in our country."

Tompkins curled his lips around one side of his chin in a snicker. "I still think they're working for the Other Side."

"Don't worry, Mr. Tompkins. If they are, Tahir will find out. He has an impeccable record."

"Yeah, but who's *he* working for?"

They could see the sign floodlit in the night.

GEOTHERMAL ENERGY STATION
EXPERIMENTAL SITE II

It stood beyond the fence amid an assembly of steel, heavy earth-drilling equipment, and rigging. A derricklike structure straddled a hole in the ground that issued gray hair wisps of steam like the sewers of New York, like their own pores exuding the nervous steam of expectation. The sign meant nothing to them — for now. They were ready to climb the forbidden mountain. The hard way.

From a mountaineering standpoint, the ascent of Ararat would ordinarily not have been an especially challenging task, and Von Parrot's southerly route to the summit could be free-climbed, that is, without the use of hardware, by anyone in a proper state of physical fitness. The nomads who by one right or another lived in the restricted zone and maintained a tent-village settlement on the southwestern slope, grazed their flocks as high as 10,000 feet, and a strong pack mule, or even a nimble goat, could climb to within a few hundred yards of the higher peak. It had not been the brutish forces of nature, but rather the eye-lowering persuasions of fear and superstition that had made most men shrink from the thought of standing higher than the Mother of the World.

Reaching the bulge in the ice on the north face was another matter, however, and while the glaciated side of Ararat was treacherous but still no Everest, getting there and back with a cat burglar's preoccupations involved the greater risk. It meant passing through the extravagantly guarded missile base unseen.

Simonian had convinced Nick and Tony that he had solved that problem, at least to the extent that they now lay under a cover of bush, prepared to follow his plan, but the climb itself presented difficulties that Nick alone foresaw might prove insurmountable.

The only way to a point on the north slope at which they could feel relatively secure that they would remain unobserved was going up through the Aghuri chasm. This was an immense cleft in the side of the mountain, a "chimney," in climber's jargon, which ran almost from top to bottom. It consisted of two sheer, vertical surfaces, at some altitudes barely wide enough for passage, and while for a climber experienced in big-wall techniques such an ascent is common, there were unavoidable limitations imposed by the need for secrecy that jeopardized the very possibility of reaching the safety zone.

Big-walling, the horizontal or vertical movement on a rise of rock or ice too steep or too smooth on which to gain a natural purchase, requires "protection," the use of specialized equipment. The variety of such aids at the climber's disposal is as rich as the recondite nomenclature used to define them, and though "bashies" can sometimes take the place of "bat hooks," and a "Clog ascender" may be preferred to a "Jumar," there is nothing on some mountain walls that can substitute for the lowly "piton." Known also as a "bong," a "lost arrow," a "turp," or simply a "nail," this is a perforated spike that can be inserted into a wall. The climber can then anchor himself to any gradient by passing his rope through a snap ring device called a "carabiner," which is attached to the eye of a piton by means of a nylon-webbing sling. In the climber's kit of metallic magic, the piton is the closest thing to an antigravity wand, but it is also useless unless driven many inches into the rock, and even Bill Forrest, mountaineering's answer to Sir Isaac Newton, has not yet conceived of the noiseless piton hammer.

When Simonian, demonstrating a consummate ignorance of technical climbing, had informed them of the need to ascend the Aghuri chasm, it was understood that to avoid detection it would have to be done silently and in the darkness of night. Both the former and the latter were remotely possible, but either, in combination with the other, was not. Yet Nick, saying nothing, studying the topographical charts of the mountain and the southing of the mid-July moon, had found a way worth a try.

In the years since he had last set foot on a slope, a revolutionary development had occurred in mountaineering, and when in his shack on the Cape of Every Little Thing he would read about it in late-arriving issues of *Summit, The American Alpine Journal,* and particularly the Sierra Club's *Ascent,* he would scoff and sneer in Sicilian, and in one unquenchable rage he almost kicked his dog. Under the intolerant pressure of the ecology movement, the once almighty piton had fallen from grace. The "Age of Ironmongery," as one indignant writer had proclaimed, was "dead." Healing the piton scars of old would have to await the winds of a thousand years, but the uglification of mountain rock had at last been condemned in the court of climbing opinion.

Nick himself had never intentionally defaced nature's sculpture, but if men had to climb mountains, that, too, was nature's way, and the Robespierrean zeal with which the trustworthy and obedient piton was being dethroned made him wonder about the human heads that would roll in the fall. To his relief, the annual publications of the American Alpine Club's *Accidents in American Mountaineering* showed no noticeably upward trends, and the sudden closing down of the great rock-hammer maker, Colorado Mountain Industries, was only a temporary failure. He had almost concluded that the self-styled purists were all bark and no bite, but he changed his mind when he read in the sports pages of the *Gazzetta di Palermo* that an Austrian team, showing up at a popular route in the California Sierras with pitons and hammers, was literally stoned by a group of "clean climbers." That was when Dobbs, biting inopportunely, nearly got booted.

Clean climbing was definitely in. It required a whole new technology, and the Merlins of mountaineering rose to the task. Ed Leeper's Antipitons and Cliff-Hanger Skyhooks; Yvon Chouinard's Hexacentric Chocks; Bill Forrest's Copperheads, Arrowheads, and Titons — one of which, weighing little more than an ounce and no larger than a quarter and a dime formed as a T, could support 4000 pounds — all these and many more permitted what was being called the pitonless "nut ascent." This meant big-walling with variously shaped nuts or chocks, usually of aluminum, that were wedged into fissures in the rock in a way that the more downward pressure applied the more they bit into the crack. Skillfully employed, they did in fact virtually eliminate the need for pitons and hammering, but they were dependent on natural fissures lying within the climber's reach, and though there are few rock walls where cracks are not in abundance, the chances of finding and assessing them in a chimney at night were nil.

Nick had calculated that the full moon would cross the Aghuri chasm that night at approximately a forty-five-degree angle, lighting the walls obliquely — which would favor the detection of cracks — for about an hour. Surveying the topography, he had also found a ledge at 9000 feet by which they could leave the Aghuri chasm, bivouac for the night, and continue the climb in the morning high enough above the military zone to risk remaining unseen. In this manner, they would have to go up the chimney only a few hundred feet, and one of the advantages of nut climbing was the conservation of one's energy, which increased the speed of ascent. Nick, who had been camming and jamming with natural and artificial chockstones as a labor-saving technique long before the "clean" climbers, felt confident in his ability to get to the ledge. Once there, he could belay his ropes from the top, permitting the others to go up by mechanical ascenders. Whether or not the moon, the rock, and a body he had abused for years would cooperate were thoughts banished from his mind.

A lone cloud passed overhead. It smeared the moonlight for a while. They watched it, saying nothing. They lay on the ground, each of them under a seventy-five-pound backpack, waiting for the base perimeter patrol, four Turkish soldiers who went by in a jeep at twenty-minute intervals. They could hear music coming from the mountain. The nomads were summoning the end-of-July storms that would replenish their pasturelands, already parched by now. It was a festival of sorts, and Simonian had informed them that it was to be expected, so it came not as a surprise, but a portent of the weather ahead. Earlier, it had occurred to Nick that the sounds might in an emergency cover the hammering of pitons, and when Simonian had remarked that the Kurds were "heathens" and the noise would be "deafening," he had brought the necessary equipment along. But the music was hardly more than the plucking of strings and the owlish hoots of primitive woodwinds, and though it traveled keenly and far in the night, it could not drown out a cough. The extra weight of the pitons pinned them down all the more.

The jeep passed. Nick and Tony began to crawl closer to the fence, but Simonian stopped them.

"Wait. There are several minutes yet."

"You sure your man can be trusted?" Nick asked him.

"Of course. He is Armenian!"

"Another cousin," Tony said to Nick.

"The only cousin I ever had," Nick replied softly, "shot my dog." He looked at his watch in the moonlight, then at one of the cranes on the other side of the fence.

Eleven

At five minutes past ten, the crane operator came out of a low concrete building. He was carrying a tool box. He entered a restricted area and was stopped by a guard. He showed him a plastic identity card, grumbled something in Turkish about how for some people even the night failed to bring rest, and he offered a cigarette. The guard, lamenting that no one had to tell him about working odd hours, glanced at the card and put the cigarette in his breast pocket. He would smoke it later, he explained, when the sergeant, lucky fellow, would be asleep. The crane operator forced himself to smile; it required a Herculean effort to be pleasant to a Turk.

He crossed the floodlit field, and checking his watch, he quickened his gait. When he reached the crane at the geothermal energy experimental site, he lifted the cowling and examined the engine with his tools. But it was all pretense, including the false identity card. Looking at the time once again, he jumped into the cab.

They heard the engine stir, belch fire, and roar.

"That, my friends," Simonian beamed, "is Grigor Missakian. The third son of my uncle's wife, on my father's side!"

The long arm of the crane came over the fence, lowering its boxlike claw. It settled easily on the ground, like a soft knock on a door. They climbed into the closed claw from the top. They began to rise, being lifted some thirty feet off the ground into the darkness above the crisscross of floodlights. They were transported over the main fence, and as prearranged by Simonian, over another that ran perpendicular to it, where they were deposited on a level grassy tract. This field was not artificially illuminated, but they could see that it had been painted, for reasons that were not immediately obvious, with white intersecting lines, forming squares about a yard by a yard. Across the field, no more than forty feet away, lay a wooded grove, and the mountain. They got out of the claw. It retracted and the arm began to retreat.

The instant he had seen the white squares, Nick sensed something was wrong, and his eyes struck out in every direction. The others were about to run for the trees, but he grabbed them both by the straps of their backpacks, and held them fast in their place.

"Don't move," he said in a harsh whisper.

They froze. He looked for the claw. It was gone. The crane engine fell silent. Only the night sounds of cicadas and the music from the mountain could be heard.

"You crazy bastard!" Nick suddenly lashed out at Simonian, filling his fists with the fabric of the Armenian's jacket.

"What the hell is wrong with you?" Tony intervened, trying to separate Nick from Simonian, who stood in dumbfounded obedience to the command to halt.

Nick took hold of Simonian's jaw like a pincer and turned his head forcibly toward the edge of the field, which was about five painted squares to one side.

"That's what's fucking wrong!"

They saw the sign: "Danger! Red Zone B! Do Not Proceed Beyond This Point Without Geometric Scheme 77/B/001!"

"This goddamn sonofabitch got us on a sonofabitching minefield! You can't cross it unless you've got the plan. That's what this chessboard is all about. And we're right in the middle of it. Fucking checkmate!"

Simonian was terrorized. "I did not know," he muttered. "It does not say . . . They did not tell us. We paid everybody. Perhaps if we walk only on the white lines . . ."

Nick was ready to lace into him again, but Tony came between them.

"Leave him!" he said. "We've got to figure out what we're going to do."

"Do?" Nick said incredulously. "I'm gonna stand right here and yell for help. That's what *I'm* gonna do!"

He turned around, as if searching for the best place to project his voice, but Tony stopped him, motioning for him to look to one side. A stubby eucalyptus rose from one of the squares about twenty feet away, and beyond that was another tree at the far rim of the minefield, both impossibly out of reach but leading to the woods. Nick knew what Tony was thinking. He began to shake his head.

"I don't like the odds. I'm yelling."

Simonian stared at them both, at a total loss. Nick raised a cupped hand to shout. Tony grabbed it.

"You know what they do to 'spies' in this country?" Tony reminded him.

Nick pulled his hand away. He began to undo his backpack. "Okay," he said. "But if you end up with your legs blown off and speaking like a goddamn choir boy, don't blame Nick Coronado."

He unreeled a long length of rope and made a lasso. The rope had a fluorescent color sheath, and as he pitched it at a low branch on the nearer tree, it looked as if he were hurling lightning. After a few tries, he ringed the branch and drew the knot tightly around it. He put on a pair of climbing mittens and gestured to the others to do the same. He explained the procedure. It was physically impossible to swing to the tree without being launched from a height, he said. The first man, himself, would take off standing on the shoulders of the second, and the second, from the shoulders of the third. Simonian blanched, asking him about the last man. Nick said he was coming to that, though only out of the goodness of his heart. The number two man, he said, would bring number three across, by climbing the tree, undoing the rope, hanging it free around a higher branch, and pulling it down with the weight of his falling body simultaneously with the third man's flight — giving him a seesaw hoist.

"Still wanna go?" Nick asked.

No one answered.

They got ready. Nick watched Simonian struggle with his backpack. Carrying three hundred pounds of flesh, bone, and gear, he looked like a hippo standing upright, and Nick doubted that he would make it across the field. Simonian appeared to agree; he was shaking. Nick shrugged and grabbed his end of the rope.

Tony hunched up to take him on, offering him the stirrup of his clasped hands for a boost. Nick got up on his shoulders, swayed one way or another for balance, and saying something to the effect that in any event they would surely meet again in the Down-Below, he swung in a grass-skimming arc to the base of the first tree.

"That was easy enough." Tony tried to reassure Simonian as they watched Nick raise himself to the branch and test it for bounce like a diving board.

Simonian merely shook his head, his lips nibbling on the edges of prayer.

The glowing rope uncoiled at their feet and snaked across the ground. Nick attempted now to ring a branch of the second tree. When he finally did, he strung the rope like a clothesline, and adopting a hand-over-hand motion, he worked his way over the field of explosives, dangling no more than four or five feet off the ground. The branches to which the line was tied strained under the weight of his body, causing him to bob up and down as if he were bouncing on a trampoline. He could feel his arm muscles stretch, a painful awakening of his old agility, and after a few loosening strokes, he moved quickly to the far side.

Tony flashed a grin and a V-sign, but Nick, aware that only a few minutes remained before the perimeter patrol would pass again, waved them on urgently, grumbling under his breath.

Simonian sweated fear, but he retained enough presence of mind to have already decided that one way or another, he would go next, believing that if the branches were weakening, his chances would be least favorable if he were last, not to speak of the more complicated task that would fall to man number three. Tony had reasoned the same way, and he was prepared to offer Simonian the advantage, deferring to his weight and age, but when he moved to hand him the rope, Simonian, misreading Tony's intent, made an unsuccessful lunge for it, swiping like a cat. Tony held the end of the rope before Simonian's pleading eyes.

"I am nervous, Tony. I want to get it over with."

"Then get it over with," Tony said, giving him the line. The word "it" came packaged with a host of meanings.

Simonian was a small planet on Tony's back, but there was time neither to complain nor assess any permanent damage. The Armenian swung. The rope slipped through his mittens, and he landed on the tentacular roots of the tree. His gasp was like the screech of rubber tearing around a curve. Nothing happened. Gathering himself together like shards, he climbed to the branch and undid the rope. He went up still higher, and following Nick's instructions, he brought Tony to the tree in a surprisingly well-coordinated movement on both sides that looked like part of a circus trapeze act. Tony nodded congratulations, and Simonian, encouraged, began the hand-over-hand movement along the tightrope.

The branches of both trees bent to extremes, groaning. The rope, digging into his meaty hands, sagged, maintaining him but an arm's length above the ground. At last, he reached the other side, tumbling into Nick's outstretched embrace, singing praises in Armenian.

Tony, observing how much pressure Simonian's weight had exerted on the support branches, had decided to switch the near end of the line to another branch, but he could hear the sound of the patrol jeep approaching, and there was no time to make such a change. Instead, he began to move swiftly along the tightrope, and had it not become slack, he might have made the crossing even faster than Nick.

About a third of the way to the far side, however, the first branch cracked, making a loud, ducklike sound. He dropped, remaining suspended only inches from the ground. He hung motionless, feeling hot blood thrust through his body driven by hammering heartbeats. He looked back. He could see the fractured branch, bent over limply, pointing almost straight downward. The illuminated rope had slipped into the crack, tightening around the finger of wood that still held the branch to the tree. He heard the jeep coming nearer. He turned toward Nick and Simonian. Simonian stared back at him with horror-struck silence, listening to the advancing patrol. Nick, however, was not in sight. Then he felt a slight tug on the rope, and he saw him up in the far tree, making hand signals that Tony failed to understand at first, but when Nick began to slowly pull in the line to take up some but not all of the slack and make chopping movements with his open hand, he got the idea.

Nick, executing a mountaineer's "aimed belay," was raising him as much as possible without putting additional strain on the remnant of broken branch, and if Tony could work his way just past the midpoint of the rope, he could cut the line and swing to safety. Gripping the rope with one hand, he removed his knife from a sheath attached to his belt, and flashed it at Nick to show that he had read the message.

Nick wound his line around a higher branch, and slid to the ground beside Simonian. Both of them held their end, as Tony, the knife handle between his clenched teeth, edged closer to them. The rope began to sag again; the knot was eating into the remains of the first branch, breaking away the hanging end. But when he reached the halfway mark, he could sense his body being taken into the orbit of the far anchor.

All of them could hear the patrol jeep stop, and the soldiers' voices. They were far enough from the main fence and the floodlit area to escape being seen, but the fluorescent rope, though not very visible at a distance, could have attracted the attention of the guards. They were, in any case, drawing nearer on foot.

"Come on!" Nick muttered under his breath, seeing Tony shifting all his strength to one hand and reaching for his knife.

He dropped it. It struck the ground directly beneath him. The soft thud stopped the soldiers in their tracks. Tony's body became rigid, as Nick and Simonian recoiled, anticipating a blast. But the knife lay in the middle of a white square, harmlessly, uselessly.

"It is a Turkish trick!" Simonian whispered fiercely. "There are no mines!"

Nick glared at him for an instant, reriveting his eyes on Tony. The soldiers moved again.

Breathing in irregular spurts, Tony continued along the line, trusting his fate now to the holding power of the broken branch. Nick, leaning over the white line that separated the minefield from the woods, extended his hands, while Simonian pulled the rope taut. Tony moved within two squares of Nick's reach. He jerked his body, whipped himself forward, and spun into Nick's arms, driving them both to the ground.

The soldiers heard the fall and began to shout. Simonian let go of the line, as Nick and Tony got to their feet. The rope unreeled wildly. The cracked branch broke off entirely, hitting the ground, and detonating a mine. It exploded violently, causing thundering echoes and rockslides on the mountain and lighting the figures of the climbers in the eyes of the guards.

The Turks cried out for them to halt, and one guard got off a rifle shot ripping blindly through the night. But they were beyond pursuit, the patrol being unprepared to cross the mine-field, and they ran deeper into the woods, their footfalls fading away.

They ran uphill on the mountain, catching their breath at the mouth of the Aghuri chasm.

A siren began to wail.

It was they, Simonian and his accomplices; Tahir felt it in his nose, and Hikmet agreed. They were with the nomads when they heard the siren and the claxon blasts of military vehicles clambering up the mountainside to the settlement. They had gone there for the music and the local color, were anyone to inquire, but really to play Simonian's game.

A freshly slain goat still twitched on a sacrificial block. The rites were reaching a crescendo, and the dark-skinned Kurds swayed like willows in the wind as a whirling dervish danced in religious ecstacy uniting with the One God to bless the shep-herds' cause. He was making rain, and though it might take days in the coming, it seemed from the perspiration that flew off his wizened skin as he reeled that he had to give up the water in his own body in the process. The Kurds stared at him hypnotically, and even the sudden presence of a contingent of armed Turkish troops could not unfix their gaze on the devo-tional kinetics of their holy man.

The soldiers moved through the crowd, fanning out in several directions. Tahir watched them with critical eyes.

"Here, they come to look," he said to Hikmet with derision.

"Where would *you* go to find white men hiding in the land of the black? In the open or in the closed? But it is better that only *I* know where they are."

Hikmet agreed.

Far-off lightning flashed in frosted panes as the dervish finished his dance, falling in a suppliant heap. Clouds had moved in to cover the moon, and the sky looked like a passing herd of whales. The faithful expected as much, and there was no outward show of exultation, only silence now that the music stopped. And in the silence, the sound of distant tapping, lasting only a moment or so before it, too, was gone. No one seemed to hear it, except Tahir, and only he knew what it was.

"They need noise," he said.

Hikmet nodded.

"But the ceremonies are over."

Hikmet nodded. Tahir thought, tugging gently on his nose. He reached into his pocket, coming up with several banknotes.

"Speak to the musicians," he told Hikmet, handing him the money. Then he looked at him queerly and took it back, adding, "Never mind. I will do it myself."

Nick idled on the wall of the Aghuri chasm like a fly. He was clipped in seventy-five feet or so higher than the others, who waited on a lip of rock for him to reach the ledge above. When the moon had been shut down on him, as if he were some sort of deadbeat, he had, recognizing the soft, andesite rock of the chasm, resorted to pitons after all. The wall was easily penetrated. With four or five light blows from his hammer, he drove them to the eye, the sounds growing higher in pitch, and though the rule was easy-in-easy-out, they could be stacked with other hardware to make them reasonably secure. But now that the cover of music was gone, he was at a standstill, and even if the moon were to reappear, too much time had been lost; the direct lighting would have passed over the chasm.

There were "go" climbs and there were "no-go" climbs, and you knew early which one you were on because everything either went right or wrong from the start, and when it was "no-go," like this one, it was saner to quit while you were still alive. Everest in '72 had been such a climb. They had barely left

Katmandu, when Ian Walker, of New Zealand, was killed; a cylinder of oxygen stored in his tent had leaked, and on the first bivouac, Walker, probably trying to light a cigarette during the night, had set himself afire. And then Monique. His whole body shook at the thought of that lousy sonofabitching oxygen tank. He was sure he had wedged the pitons wrong and he was going to fall. He felt the chasm closing in on him, tightening like a vise. Then the music started up again, louder than ever.

It was routine now. He climbed to the ledge with his old speed, or something close to it, driving his pitons to a familiar beat. Apparently the nomads had not been insulated from some Western influence. Still he found it strange that now that the serious business was over, the musicians were either amusing themselves or someone who liked "Tenderly," "As Time Goes By," and other hits of the forties. Nick, belaying his rope from above, caught himself humming "Mairzy Doats."

With the main anchor point belayed at the top, for the others the climb had been reduced to a beginner's task. Simonian made a "magnanimous" gesture for Tony to go first, as if in atonement for his earlier display of cravenness, but Tony understood it was only more of the same. If anything were to go wrong, it would occur as a result of the lead climber's faulty technique, and it would be more likely to happen on the first try than on the second.

Tony attached himself to the line, linking the top rope, which threaded through the pitons and chocks that gripped the wall, to the harness already buckled to his body — a system of webbing designed to distribute the shock of a fall caught by the rope equally around the torso. Operating a hand-held ascending device, which was clamped to the rope and resembled a stapling gun, he swung into the chasm, getting a toehold on the wall. He began to maneuver himself upward. A buoying wave of exhilaration seemed to be lifting him. His pack felt at one with his body. Pressing downward for purchase with the blunt ends of his boots, he learned quickly how to maintain a momentum that made him soar like a diver surfacing from the deep. He felt almost weightless. He had climbed before: Sunday rock climbs at Cragmont, the Grizzly Caves, and Miraloma. He knew the correct use of hand- and footholds, belays, and friction brake rappels — but he had never big-walled, and now he understood why others did. It was the conquest of gravity, not rock, that excited him with the feeling of being released from an eternal drag, the Spoiler who had tripped his very first baby steps, who pulled ruinously on his skin and bones and bodily organs, who in one final malignity would bring him down for all time.

He could see Nick leaning over the ledge, and he was about to fire a triumphant grin when one of the pitons dislodged. The wall shoved him into the void, but he dropped only two feet as the top belay drew taut. His harness tightened around him. It was not an uncomfortable feeling, rather more like a reassuring embrace. But he hung too far from the wall to regain a foothold, not knowing exactly what to do, and Nick was no help: he stared at him as if he had already been swallowed by the gorge.

"Hey," Tony called to him, swaying lightly from side to side, "are you all right?"

The paradox in his voice shook Nick back to life. He took hold of the rope, which had been digging into the angle of the ledge, and pulled Tony close to the wall. Now, Tony could continue as before, and he came over the top, falling safely into Nick's grasp.

Nick clutched him tightly, burying his face to hide his emotion. Tony felt Nick's body rattle once, before he pulled away.

"I guess it happened the same way," Tony said softly.

Nick tried to answer, but all he could do was clear his throat and nod his head.

Simonian's voice came up through the chasm. "Everything is in order?"

"Yeah," Nick called down to him, "peaches and cream."

Twelve

They spoke about it later. Simonian had come up as slow as grass but without mishap. They had eaten "big-wall food," better known as salami, and Nick had made tea on a mountaineer's high-altitude grasshopper stove, but Simonian, showing the first symptoms of the rarefied oxygen environment, had fallen asleep on his backpack before the drink had been brewed. It was quiet now. The moon had broken through again, and the lightning had used up all the electric in the air and would have to await another day. The stars shone, and being a little closer to them here, they seemed bigger than usual in the tarry sky. The nomads dreamed of rain.

Nick heated more tea, and when he poured it into his tin cup, he spiked it with cognac. Tony had the same.

"It's not unusual," Nick said, out of nowhere. His hand shook as he put the cup to his lips. "A fall like yours, I mean. Only some wise sonofabitch had bought used rope because the good stuff was getting to cost a dollar a foot then, and he got it for half that. Well, there's nothing wrong with used rope unless it's caught some bad falls. I guess this one had. Anyway, it snapped. I held her. God, I held her. Then I couldn't hold her and she was gone. No scream. Nothing. She fell about a mile." He poured more cognac, less tea. Tony nursed his drink.

"I went down for her. Took me hours. It was night when I found the body. It was perfect. No blood. No bruises. She'd fallen into a cushion of new snow. Maybe it didn't even kill her.

By the time I got to her, she'd turned to ice." He closed his eyes. "A beautiful statue. With this funny look in her eyes. Like she'd forgot her keys, or missed a train, or some dumb thing like that . . ." He looked up at Tony, suddenly sorry he had opened an attic window on his soul. "Ah, what am I telling you all this for?"

"Maybe you need someone to talk to."

"Me? I don't need fucking anything, kid."

"Except money."

Nick shot a mean glance at him. "Yeah, money. You wouldn't know about that, would you?"

Tony was noncommittal in his expression.

"You know what I did after I quit climbing?" Nick said, filling his cup again. "Rescue. Saving amateurs who get stuck on the Alps. Flying choppers and all that. I did it for the money. Only business was slow. The resort owners didn't like it. It's a great big tourist attraction, looking through a telescope at frozen corpses high on a mountain from your hotel window."

"I take it you don't think much of the human race."

"The human race is fucking fine, kid. It's the people who stink."

Tony smiled. Nick sipped his tea, to hide his own smile. They both noticed that his hands were trembling, and he extended them defiantly.

"Wanna turn back?"

"We'll be all right."

Nick appreciated the confidence. He put the bottle of cognac away.

"How'd you ever get into this archaeology thing, anyway?" He sounded almost friendly.

"If I told you, you'd probably laugh," Tony said hesitantly.

"Yeah, I probably would."

They heard something heavy drop, not the crash of falling rock, but something soft and limp. They got up and ran in the direction of the sound. A human body, cloaked in a burnoose, lay face down on the ground. Nick turned it around. Tony drew back, startled. It was Hoffmann, ashen in the moonlight, dead.

Tony scampered up a crag, chasing rustling noises in the dark.

"Wait!" Nick cried, but Tony was gone. He had seen the look of recognition in Tony's eyes, and now he stared after him, muttering, "Dumb kid."

Simonian had been awakened by the commotion. He came up to Nick, bleary-eyed, then shocked at the sight of the dead man. Nick told him what had happened.

"Perhaps Tony is keeping something from us," Simonian said.

"Maybe you too. What's up there, Simonian?"

Simonian smiled. "The ark of the great Patriarch is not enough for you, Coronado?"

"It's hard to split three ways."

"Yes. Unfortunately the spoils of Ararat are indivisible. But I am just a simple guide. You must keep your eyes on Tony. Do you not agree?"

"One eye, Simonian. One on him. One on you."

Simonian roared, his echo moving rocks.

When Tony returned he went through Hoffmann's cloak, explaining who he was. He found nothing.

"Did you see anything up there?" Nick asked him.

He nodded. "Something big. Moving faster than I could. Fleetly, like an animal. On two legs."

He examined the body. It was as cold as the night air, and the skin had a uniform pallor that seemed oddly colorless even for a corpse. He knew that Hoffmann had been dead for at least a day, and he lifted the extremities looking for dark splotches where the blood would have settled, but none were visible. Then he discovered why: there was a deep, scab-covered wound on the upper part of the chest between the collar bones, and a punctured artery protruded from the opening like a piece of rubber hose; Hoffmann had bled to death.

He flaked away the blackened scab. He saw teeth marks, the same flat, regular semicircles that Sippara's bite had shown. *Kehli.*

"It was a bear," Simonian said. "There are bears on Ararat, you know."

"Bears don't run on two legs," Nick said.

Tony was silent. He wished he had paid more attention to his courses on the history of religions; that was where he had learned about metempsychosis.

Resident Agent Franklin Tompkins was summoned to his codex telephone at eight o'clock the next morning to receive a call from Washington; more precisely, from the home office in Langley, Virginia.

He had been asleep in his quarters on the base, but trained as he was to respond with a fireman's alacrity, it took only minutes for him to dress, rush to another wing of the building, and arrive at his end of the line looking none the worse for it, except for the one brown sock that did not match the one black, or vice versa. In any case, they were hidden under his trousers, and no one would be the wiser, least of all Langley, Virginia.

Waiting for the call to come through, he inserted his codex identity component, a waferlike, solid-state electronic tab, into a slot in the phone, and he began to shave with an electric razor. He had no notion of what the message might be, though it certainly was of major importance. (Were they upping his priority yet another notch?) A communication of this nature was a highly unusual event, unprecedented, in fact, although the equipment had been installed for weeks.

In the first place, the telephone — even one that could only be used by the person in possession of the codex component, and one that could signal-scramble past any known bugging device — was a fundamentally untrustworthy instrument, to be employed only in the most special circumstances. You could never be absolutely sure that the person with whom you were speaking was not an imposter, a voice impersonater from the Other Side, and while like most agents, Tompkins always — even when he slept, bathed, and engaged in concupiscent activities that required bodily contact with other human beings — wore his codex ID dangling from a chain around his neck like a symbol of one's religion, there had been cases where the tab had been separated from its owner, most often immediately after the chain had been used to effect an abrupt, unscheduled demise.

In the second place, the time difference between the TMZ and the eastern seaboard of the United States, eight and a half hours, meant that the caller was telephoning in the middle of the Langley night. (Were they upping it *two* notches?) Tompkins, who had spent much of his adult life abroad, was proud of his learned ability to make instant conversions, no matter where on the globe he might be, into Eastern Standard or Daylight Time. He had developed his own technique, and its main advantage was that arithmetical computations, which so frequently resulted in errors, were entirely unnecessary. If, for example, it was four P.M. in Central Europe, which was normally six hours ahead of Langley, you had only to close your eyes and picture a clock, then draw an imaginary straight line that passed through the center of the dial to the other side and read the number there; thus, without adding or subtracting it could only be ten A.M. at home. At Ararat, the method was only slightly more complex. You used the same image as for Central Europe, but since the TMZ was two and a half hours later still, when you saw the diametral number, you "pushed" the envisioned hands of the clock to where they ought to be.

Tompkins, when he had finished shaving, looked at his watch. It was 8:20 A.M. He shut his eyes tightly and Big Ben appeared inside the lids. (He could have conjured up any timepiece, of course, but he always used the London tower's clock because the numerals were so easily read.) He straight-lined to the other side. He "pushed." It was 4:50 A.M. in Langley, he thought, and he could see a pink-lemonade dawn breaking over Virginia. (It would be *highest* priority, for sure.)

Actually, it was ten minutes to midnight in eastern United States, and the sun had set only three hours before. Not that there was anything basically wrong with Tompkins's time-calculating system; the trouble was that whenever he had to "push," he could never remember whether to go forward or in reverse, and anyway, he was right about one thing: the call was exceedingly momentous.

The telephone rang. The party at the other end was Tompkins's immediate superior, recently appointed to replace his predecessor, who had been killed in the line of duty in a mysterious accident on Joannøja, a remote island high above the Arctic Circle. The new man had been a field agent for many years at a rank equal to Tompkins's, and they had often worked together, so the conversation between them began quite informally.

"How's it goin, ol' buddy?" Tompkins asked, feeling a tinge of disappointment that the call had not come from higher up. "They gettin' you desk fellas up at the crack of dawn these days ... or are you just buckin' to be big dog in the meat house?"

Tompkins, sensing an incipient note of superiority in his superior's voice, took a briefing on the correct time, and realizing at once that he had "pushed" in the wrong direction, he quickly let the matter drop. He listened carefully to instruction, growing increasingly skeptical that his priority would be raised at all.

"You can't do this to me!" he cried out when he began to perceive at least part of what was wanted of him. "We're only seventy-two hours from the test, and we've got a whole village of Kurdos to evacuate. I can't have NASA and Pentagon brass on my neck wanting the grand tour, ol' buddy! ... Okay. 'Sir.' But anyway, the Tillies'll never stand for it. ... Who? ... *Him?* ... You wouldn't shit — I mean, is that the God's honest truth? ... Well, of course, I'll do everything I can, ol' — sir."

Tompkins hung up, reflecting on the thin bond of buddy-buddy relationships. Then his mind drifted. *Him,* he thought, gosh all Friday. There was a knock at the door. It was Colonel Hakim Hakim.

"There is a serious problem, Mr. Tompkins," he said.

Tompkins, who could envisage no problem more pressing than the one whose resolution had been entrusted to him by *him,* tried his best to crack through the colonel's sobriety. He offered him a cigarette, a Marlboro. Hakim Hakim refused, but Tompkins carried on.

"Yeah, Hakim, ol' buddy, there sure is. Say, I never asked you. How do you like to be called? By your first name, or your last name?" He guffawed, lighting a Marlboro. Hakim Hakim was stony. "Look, colonel, Washington wants ... uh ... would like —"

Hakim Hakim raised his hand for him to say no more. "We already know."

Tompkins looked at him icily. Was it possible that the Tillies had found a way to tap the untappable? "Know?" he asked nonchalantly.

"Your State Department has been in touch with Ankara. We shall have to receive your . . . 'observers.' But that is merely an inconvenience, not the problem." Hakim Hakim lit a Turkish cigarette, a Fez. "Simonian and the others," he went on, "they have vanished. They passed through one of the red zones last night. A very professional incursion. Now, they can only be on the mountain."

Tompkins worried. If anything were to go wrong while the brass would be present, it would undoubtedly get back to *him*. "What about that clown from Istanbul?" he snapped. "He was supposed to keep them under surveillance."

The door opened. Tahir entered with a smile that widened as Tompkins reddened. Hikmet trailed behind him.

"The clown from Istanbul," Tahir announced, "merely shrugs his shoulders and says be patient."

"Look, Tahir," Tompkins fired, "I don't buy your Sherlock Holmes act!"

"A pity. But, I have good news for you, 'major.'" Tahir raised a philosophical finger. "Whatever goes up, must come down."

Tompkins bought that one. He stroked his chin and nodded. He sat and crossed his legs, exposing a brown sock. "Yeah," he said tugging on his trousers, "I guess we got 'em by the short hairs, don't we? And anyway, they'll have a big surprise coming, if they don't come down by the time we go with the test. It's suicide, right Hakim, ol' buddy?"

Tahir turned to Hakim Hakim, who nodded solemnly. Tahir, who was only vaguely familiar with the test program, realized that he had underestimated this factor. He walked to a window that faced the geothermal energy station. A pile driver in the drilling rig pounded rhythmically, shrouded in slowly escaping steam.

Tompkins no longer worried, but Tahir did.

Thirteen

Following a natural trail, the climbers ascended without much difficulty except for the effects of the weight of their backpacks in the thinning atmosphere and the ubiquitous thorns that tore at their clothes and their flesh. Apart from the bush, the ground wore a hand-me-down gown of withering grass trimmed with tiny flowers too weak to give off their own color. Juniper flapped its wings in a morning breeze. The sun pumped in a dark blue sky. The snow line was a mile above them, and though the temperature was freezing there, and baking on the plain below at their present altitude it was invigoratingly in-between.

Nick, completely at home in the mountain environment, led the way. He moved heel first, as if the terrain were as flat as a boardwalk, and every now and then he stopped to examine a rock or pick a wild berry, permitting the others to catch up. Tony, wearing down the balls of his feet, did a fair job at keeping the pace. Simonian stumbled along, cursing cantankerously, falling further and further afield.

"Tougher than you thought?" Nick asked Tony when they had stopped for a moment's rest, waiting for Simonian to close the gap.

"The story of my life. I'm waiting for an elevator that's going to take me someplace important. Finally, the doors slide open, and there's a long, endless flight of steps going up."

"Same with me, kid. Only there's nothing important."

Nick started upward again, but he heard the pile-driving sound rising from below, and he moved to an overhang for a look.

From a standstill at 9000 feet, the fenced-in base was like a box where a child keeps his toys. The underground silos, loaded with nuclear warheads, seemed the mere muzzles of dart guns. An erector-set rig, carved into the side of the mountain, was drilling into the ground. Nick waited for the others to reach him, then he turned to Simonian questioningly. "Oil?"

"Water. Boiling water. They think there are rivers of it under the ground. If they find it, it comes up like a tea kettle, and whoof, they make cheap electricity. That is what the 'big' operations are all about on the twentieth. It is a test."

Both Nick and Tony looked at him with surprise. They had planned their return for the twentieth. Simonian had claimed to have reliable information that the whole southwest area was scheduled to be entirely evacuated of all the nomads and base personnel because of some sort of military "maneuvers" that would last all that day, and that they would therefore be able to return unobserved, obviating the need to pass through the base again. At the time it had sounded reasonable enough, but now the notion of a test implied an uncalculated risk.

"How do we know the 'tea kettle' won't go off in our face?" Nick asked.

"You saw the steam by the cranes," Simonian said. "Little gray hairs. We will not be within a mile of it."

"So why are they clearing the whole hillside?" Nick went on.

Simonian laughed scoffingly, wiping sweat from his brow. "It is a *very* important 'military secret.' "

"No more minefields, Simonian?" Tony asked.

"Believe me, Tony. Our troubles are over. On the twentieth we will walk through — with news of the ark."

Nick looked up at the peak above them. Great Ararat, a purple white, broad-shouldered dome, rose like an enemy fortress.

On the Plain of Igdir, the midday sun was a skillet of frying fat. The earth was the color and texture of a hundred-year-old newspaper, as shriveled and dry as a roasted peanut, and the air was as thick as sand. Tahir, however, sat in a clearing by the side of the mountain, playing backgammon with Hikmet, while Dobbs got a suntan on his tongue. True, the inspector was in the shade of a faded umbrella, drinking Fanta orangeade; he wore a handkerchief tucked into his collar for a sweat band, and he fanned himself with the brim of his hat, but if the elements were conspiring to try his patience, they, like the pollen and the underworld, were learning a thing or two.

He had been there for hours, training a pair of high-powered binoculars on the mountain from time to time between dice throws, catching glimpses of the climbers all morning long. But he had lost sight of them for a while now, and Hikmet had taken over the job.

"Think, Hikmet," Tahir said wryly, "there is only the ark between them and . . ." He lifted his eyes to the heavens.

Hikmet raised an agnostic brow over the eyepieces of the glasses. He was thinking that there was only a six-pack of Fanta between himself and starvation.

"You are right," Tahir said, knowing what Hikmet was thinking. "It is the lunch hour. Perhaps that is why we cannot find them." He stood. "We will go to the commissary. They say you can watch the drilling from there. Who knows? Perhaps our government will find the ark by drilling. In the Byzantine bureaucracy, one always starts from the bottom."

He laughed three times and put on his hat. Hikmet, showing a special appreciation of the inspector's remark, laughed once. Dobbs ran toward the mountain, then turned and barked at Tahir.

Nick had gone through a narrow pass exploratorily and was considerably ahead of the others when the biting creature pounced on him like a jaguar. It threw him to the ground, trying to sink its teeth in a jugular vein.

The beast had come from behind, dropping from a height, digging its nails into his shoulders and the sides of his calves. Nick had gone down striking his chin on a rock, and now, twisting out of its clutches, they were eye to eye. He saw what was, or once had been, a man.

He had long, red, knotted hair and a matted red beard that flared like solar prominences around a mouth that growled. His teeth were sharp and as polished as river stones. He flashed them territorially, exposing them to the inflamed ridges of his gums like a wolf protecting his lair. His body was swathed in hides. His finger- and toenails were twice any normal length; the protruding ends were stiff, pinched, and curved, like a cat's. He had Caucasian features and a fair-skinned face that was boyishly freckled, though he looked at least fifty years old.

Nick, recovering from the initial shock, spun out from under and got to his feet, retreating until he had slipped out of his backpack. He saw no reason to attempt flight. Now that the savage had lost the element of surprise, Nick was confident that he could subdue him, and he detected fear in his assailant's pale blue eyes. The man was frail and undoubtedly grossly undernourished, and though he continued to bare his formidable teeth, he seemed to sense that he was decisively outmatched.

"It's all right, friend," Nick said soothingly. "No one wants to hurt you."

The man's eyes widened. He opened his mouth as if to speak, but could manage only a raspy grunt. Nick took a cautious step toward him, as one might approach a frightened child. Suddenly, however, the man scooped up a pointed rock and charged. Nick let him come, stepping aside, and ramming his fist into the man's gut, doubling him up as he passed. Nick leaped on him, readying a blow at his jaw, but the man, heaving foul smelling air, was already too weakened to offer any further resistance. He stared at Nick with a pathetic plea in his eyes, passing out in Nick's arms.

Tony rushed up, struck with incredulity at what he saw, and before he could utter a word, they heard a dull thump. The man was torn from Nick's hold and thrown back to the ground.

A few drops of blood oozed from a hole freshly drilled through the man's forehead and something he was wearing around his neck fell out from under his hides. Nick and Tony looked around. Simonian stood behind them holding his .357 Magnum equipped with a silencer. It was still raised in a firing position. They stared at the weapon. Simonian grinned.

"It is good you did not cry out, Coronado." He patted the silencer affectionately. "As you know, sound carries terribly here."

"He was unconscious!" Nick cried in a fury.

"Good. He did not suffer."

Tony was white with rage. "You said no guns, Simonian!"

Simonian held the Magnum at a serviceable angle. "I said no noise, Tony."

Tony bent over the body of the red-headed savage.

"He's no Turk," Nick said.

Kehli, Tony thought. "His name," he said softly, "is Kelly."

They looked at him curiously, but Tony made no reply. He showed them the man's necklace, running his fingers lightly over the glistening surface of a string of human teeth.

All afternoon they searched for Kelly's cave. When they found it, under a natural canopy of rock, not very far from where they had begun, they had completely circled the Great Ararat cone, having made no upward progress at all. It was dusk, a day lost and done, but after Tony had expressed his belief that they were under a threat from an arcane, hostile religious cult that had captured and had somehow animalized Kelly, it seemed imperative that they investigate further. From that aspect, Nick and Tony were thankful that Simonian was armed, though they found no sign of other human life.

Bulbous clouds had been forming for hours, and the tumescent evening sky hung closely over their heads, as if from meat hooks. It looked like an awful bruise, with gashes of lightning far more severe than the night before. A muddy darkness settled swiftly, and not until they had got a fire going could they begin to explore Kelly's cave.

It was a house of horrors or a child's nightmare. The light flickered on sweating walls. Curtains of cobwebs crossed every angle, and the adhesive dust of broken webs carpeted the floor. Hides had been strung like clothes on a line, and animal bones were scattered everywhere. They were heaped in corners, stuck into crevices, and strewn randomly about, some cracked, some pulverized, and those that were not yet dry and picked clean were covered with insect swarms. The pungent smell of decaying organic matter permeated the cave, worsening as one went deeper inside, where bats, driven back by the light, slammed against the walls. The shed skins of snakes crackled like cellophane under every footfall.

The cave was shaped like a trumpet, and where the firelight failed and only darkness lay beyond, a narrow tunnel began, but when Tony struck a match, they got a glimpse of more of the same. Nick and Simonian retreated. It seemed prudent to guard their rear, and Simonian took up a vigil at the entrance to the cave, while Nick prepared the evening meal.

Tony returned several minutes later, hauling a battered old piece of luggage by a length of frayed rope tied around the handle. He confirmed that the tunnel offered no new surprises — apart from the contents of the suitcase. Simonian stared at it with a strange intensity. He drew his gun, and began to polish the muzzle with a handkerchief.

"You have looked inside?" he asked nervously.

"Yes. His name was Kelly all right. Michael J. Kelly. And he lived in Paterson, New Jersey. A long time ago. Did you know him, Simonian?"

Simonian shifted the Magnum to his right hand, slipping the handkerchief into his pocket. "I have a bad memory for names. Perhaps there is a photograph inside, before he grew his fur."

Tony shook his head. "I didn't see any photos." He opened the rusty latches. "This is where he kept his valuables."

The Armenian took a bracing step back from both of them as Tony raised the lid. Nick was stunned by what he saw, but Simonian, though he too expressed astonishment, appeared to ease somewhat.

Three human skulls, in a nest of damp, rotting papers and various other objects, stared back at them with eyeless darkness. Christian names were painted in red on the frontal bones: Jimmy, Frank, Chuck. They were more or less intact and otherwise indistinguishable from one another, except one, "Jimmy," was toothless.

Simonian sat on a rock and returned to cleaning his gun. Both he and Nick watched with awed silence as Tony removed Jimmy from the case, holding it by the mandible and occipital bones to prevent it from swinging on the jaw hinges. He ran his fingers over the painted name, scraping some of it with his nail, and rubbing the flaked substance between his fingertips until it powdered.

"It's not nail polish," he said.

He opened the jaw and tried several of the teeth strung on Kelly's necklace, inserting them in the proper sockets. They fit.

"I guess Jimmy was Kelly's favorite," Nick said.

Tony showed them the cranium of the skull painted Frank.

"Frank has a cracked parietal bone. He must have been killed with a rock."

"Or in a fall," Nick said.

"Ah," Simonian reflected, "the lure of the ark is great."

"Maybe," said Tony, laying the skulls side by side. "And maybe they were lured by something else." He opened all the jaws and hung the necklace over the edge of the valise. "The same kind of sloppy dental work," he said pointing to teeth in each of the dentitions, "as though they all used the same incompetent dentist."

"The fucking army!" Nick blurted.

"The United States fucking Army," Tony corrected. He reached into the case and came up with four sets of U.S. military dogtags dangling from beaded metal chains. "These men were all born more than fifty years ago. When they were in the army, it must have been during World War Two, or soon afterward."

Nick turned to Simonian. "Wasn't that about the time you were 'helping' the Americans, Simonian?"

"You are correct," he replied indignantly. "We were building the airfield to supply the Armenian freedom fighters. But one does not make runways on a mountain, Coronado."

"Was there any talk of climbing...for Noah's ark, of course?"

"Talk? There is always talk. Too much talk, Coronado." He paused and peered down the gunsight of the Magnum in a not-so-idle gesture meant to emphasize that he alone was armed. "But I do not know these men. We must ask the serpent people who they are."

"Too bad old Kelly died," Nick said sardonically. "He might have saved us the trouble."

They ate in a few silent minutes. Nick unrolled his sleeping bag, and saying that there was a lot of hill to climb tomorrow, he sacked in by the fire.

Simonian said that it was impermissible for an Armenian to sleep in the presence of the dead, but Nick and Tony understood. Now that they knew he had a gun, he felt the need to protect it from falling out of his control. He would either have to conceal it or find a hiding place to pass the night — every night. He began to move his gear outdoors, slowly, waiting for Nick to fall asleep, as if to forestall conspiracy, but that only took a minute or two and he left.

Tony continued to go through the contents of Kelly's suitcase. The papers were laden with grease, and as a result, transluscent. It was apparent from impressions on the pages that they had once been filled with hand-written notes, but not a word remained legible, and Tony knew this had been caused by the solubility of pencil graphite in animal fat, or human.

He held several sheets to the light, and though he could see that the writing had been scrawled wildly, uphill and downhill, and curved around corners to form arabesque borders, he could make out no more than the fiercest exclamation marks and a great deal of frenetic crossing out.

There were four other objects in the case: a leadless pencil worn to a cigarette-butt length; a knife with a serpent handle; a copy of the *Black Writing* in Kirmanji; and a wooden paddle that looked like a table-tennis racquet with writing on both sides. Hand-lettered with a substance that had resisted corrosion, it was a kind of catechism consisting of short, easily memorized English sentences: the dogma of the serpent people. One side reproduced a biblical type of genealogy. It read:

These are the generations of the Superior Power.

The Serpent is the Member of the Superior Power and Eve was his concubine.

Cain is derived from the Superior Power and he went east of Eden and became the first nomad.

Abel and the House of Seth are derived from the inferior power.

Lamech is derived from the Superior Power and Cain's revenge is seven fold but Lamech's revenge is seventy and seven fold.

Noah is derived from the inferior power but he preserved the knowledge of good and evil and he is with us.

Ham is derived from the Superior Power and he is the chief of the Kenites after the flood.

The Shinarites, the Sodomites, and the Gomorrahns are derived from the Superior Power and their revenge is seven hundred and seventy and seven fold.

Esau is derived from the Superior Power and he was cheated of his birthright, and became the chief of the Edomites.

The Edomites were brethren to the Kenites and they mined copper and iron.

The Edomites and the Kenites were brethren to the Zealots and the Sicarii and they were all derived from the Superior Power.

Judas of the Sicarii, or Judas Iscariot, destroyed the false messiah freeing mankind of Jesus Christ.

The other side was doctrine:

The Serpent gave mankind knowledge of good and evil, withheld by the inferior power.

Cain taught men to rebel against the inferior power.

Noah preserved knowledge of good and evil and he is with us.

The Shinarites, Sodomites and Gomorrahns, the Kenites, Edomites, Zealots, and Sicarii taught men to form nations and rebel against the inferior power.

Judas Iscariot freed mankind of Jesus Christ.

The Superior Power rises. He is the Son of the Morning.

His revenge is seven thousand and seven hundred and seventy and seven fold seven times.

The Superior Power is the Morning Star.

Tony read the tablets several times, his skin taking on a film of perspiration as if he had fallen into an oil barrel of blasphemy. At first it seemed odd to him that, in a territory dominated by Islam, these people should be so concerned with Judeo-Christian themes, but the academic acquaintance he had with the Koran reminded him of its echoes of the Bible, and that Muhammad himself believed that he was a successor to Abraham and Jesus. He realized, too, however, that these statements could in no way be a translation of Muslim polemical writings. Islam does not admit the dualistic idea of superior and inferior powers, and if the "House of Seth" were derived from the latter, that would mean that Muhammad, like Abraham and Jesus, was also so derived. Abel was childless when he was murdered, and in the genealogy of the Bible, there were only two "houses" that emerged from the Garden of Eden, that of Seth, which gave the world all of the Genesis Patriarchs, Moses, David, Jesus and Muhammad, and that of the primal killer, Cain.

The House of Good and the House of Evil, Tony thought, and here on Ararat they had entered the spiritually sordid kingdom of the latter. There was much he did not know, but his studies of ancient civilizations, which had given him a scholarly grasp of the Bible, made him understand that this was the religion of the damned, the revenge-lusting faith of all who had been "wronged" by the "inferior power" — God.

For giving Eve the omnipotence of the gods, the Serpent, or the Member, was condemned to wallow in dust and an eternity of slithering lowliness; for offering God the fruit of the soil, Cain, the orgasmic spurt of the Superior Power himself, was driven to desperation. The reference to the Shinarites, Tony knew, could only mean the fallen builders of the Tower of Babel, who by speaking one language had discovered how to do whatever they had a mind to, and the Sodomites and the Gomorrahns were all slain, wicked or not. He knew little of the Edomites, other than that Esau, by guile and deception, had twice been outwitted by his favored brother. The Kenites were a pariah people, he recalled, though he could not think of why, and he found it curious, in view of the satellite's detection of metals in the Ararat ice cap, that the catechism made a point of noting that both the Kenites and the Edomites mined copper and iron. He could remember nothing that could be said in behalf of Judas, but if he really had been a member of the Zealots and Sicarii, as the name Iscariot seemed to imply, it was conceivable that the betrayal might be regarded by them as Christ's, not his; Jesus and the Zealots and Sicarii had enemies in common, namely the Pharisees and Sadducees, and at least one of the Apostles was a Zealot; the Sicarii were activists with strong politico-religious ambitions, and if Judas believed Jesus to be their political Messiah, it was as inevitable that he would be disappointed as he would be impelled to do something about it.

How all this had come to form a system of mystical beliefs for an obscure clan of nomads in western Asia, Tony could only guess. Like Cain, they bore the curse of being forced to wander, and Noah, who was with them, who had preserved the Serpent's knowledge of good and evil, seemed to be their only link with the Superior Power, whose passion for vengeance 7777 seven times over they surely shared. He had perceived from Sippara that they worshipped Noah, and the animalizing of Kelly, however perversely achieved, was undoubtedly the expiation of sin. Had Kelly, and his fellow followers of the inferior power, cast profaning eyes on the ark, sullying a sacred shrine? The unanswerable questions formed in his mind like words being chiseled on stone.

In the end, sliding helplessly into a viper pit of sleep, tormented by the preying shadows of what he might dream, he felt sure of one thing alone. He knew who the Superior Power was. The Son of Morning and the Morning Star are one — Lucifer.

All those unlucky sevens, he thought, sinking into the reptilian sea, and this was a seventh year.

Fourteen

They began again at dawn, setting their sights at the snow line 2000 feet above, with the goal of reaching it by twilight. They climbed in a steep ravine that formed a winding passage to the ice cap. It was ankle-deep with swiftly flowing water running off from the melting snow, and when the sun burned through the morning haze opening the sky like a furnace door, the water rose into a torrent of rapids. It hurled slabs of ice in their path, and boulders of black detritus rock turned loose by the melt raced past them like a mounted horde. Soon they were in a hip-high river of icy waters. It numbed them to the marrow and it roared a war.

Nick had known it would be like this. Mountains are regular, relieving their bowels in the first heat of morning of matter frozen fast at night. A seasoned climber waits — when there's time. They had roped themselves together, for there was a danger of any one of them being swept away, and each forward step required the marshaling of all the strength in every muscle and cunning calculation. They advanced at a crippled pace using their long-handled ice axes as walking sticks, but more often they could do no more than cling to the gully wall and deflect the onslaught of debris that came at them like body blows from a winning fighter's fists.

By noon, however, their altimeter told them that they had crept 800 feet, and feeling they had learned how much Mount Ararat could hate, they hoisted themselves onto a narrow shelf of rock, laying their exhaustion in the sun.

Tahir had watched for them in vain all morning with his binoculars. Now he found them perched on the overhang a quarter of a mile below the snow line. He lowered the glasses and smiled at Hikmet, who was devouring a picnic lunch.

"They are safe," Tahir proclaimed.

Hikmet offered him the basket of food, throwing his scraps to Dobbs. But Tahir refused. He plucked a wild flower from the ground instead and breathed its fragrance deeply. Hikmet stared at him with surprise, expecting an echoing sneeze. Even Dobbs looked up from his crumbs and cocked his head in anticipation. But the scent had no ill effect.

"The rewards of patience," Tahir remarked. He returned to his binoculars. Then his face took on a sudden gravid look. "They are not safe," he said, gazing intently at the distant climbers.

Tahir had seen what Nick was first to hear. They had all been asleep when the low rumble began, and it was lost in the thundering rush of water. But the sound grew loud, and when Nick's eyes shot open, he could already feel the trembling. He scarcely had to look up to know that they were in the path of an avalanche of ice and rock.

He shook the others awake. They leaped to their feet, but there was no time to escape. They had no recourse but to remain where they were and hand their fate to the hat-check girl of fortune. The ledge jutted out about three or four feet over an abyss, and the wall behind them stood no more than ten feet high. They pressed themselves to it as thin as they possibly could, face first so that their backpacks might act as a cushion when the slide would go over their heads like a waterfall.

A whole Niagara of slush and stone was suddenly above them. They threw up their hands as a shield, but that was only blind reflex; some of the boulders that flew by were large enough to crush them to a sticky splatter. Riding on smaller rocks, the boulders were flung into the emptiness below as they came screaming over the wall, but many of them struck the ledge as they fell, chipping it away. The climbers were pelted with pebble-sized stones and a cascade of melted snow, and the platform they stood on steadily shrank to almost nothing at all.

The mountain itself seemed to be coming apart or seized with a convulsive frenzy. It shook violently, like a dog out of water, as if it were trying to throw the alien beings from its walls, and when at last its rage was spent, and the climbers had crawled to safety, it added insult to injury, vomiting the ledge itself into the void.

No one spoke. They started upward through the rapids once more, as angry as the mountain, as angry as the storm clouds blackening the afternoon sky.

Franklin Tompkins, his mission priority upped two whole notches, stood under the troubled sky with his palm stretched out like a Gypsy's. He held it flat, rigid, and parallel to the ground lest anyone think him gay. He was with Colonel Hakim Hakim and a small reception party waiting on the apron of the base airfield for the VIPs to arrive. His reddish hair was tossed by the wind so that it looked like a bowl of *spaghetti al pomodoro*. He was testing for the first drops of rain. He had a theory, gained through life experience, that the mood of visiting brass was invariably determined by the weather that had accompanied their journey, and he hoped that this brass would not be delayed by the impending storms. And what brass they were!

When the notch-raising Telex had arrived that morning, it had also disclosed the names of the "observers." He was astonished to see that apart from a four-star general, two full colonels, and a special assistant to the director of NASA, also due to arrive was the man from the State Department known in Washington and in foreign diplomatic circles by his initials alone, RMS.

Indeed, few people could tell you his full name, and though Tompkins was one of the few, he could never quite remember whether the M stood for Millington or Millingsworth — or was it Mellingsworth or Mellington, or some other similar syllabic construction? Everyone on the inside, however, was aware that RMS, not the Secretary, was the real power at State, and some even made the same claim with regard to the White House, too. In any case, he had been personally installed by the President, after yielding to pressure applied by his party to deny RMS the nominally top job at State, since it was questionable that the Senate would ever consent. RMS, from boyhood on the President's closest friend, had once, in a moment of spiritual rebirth, declared in an interview with the *New York Review of Books* that in his heart of hearts he had often committed unorthodox carnal acts — the reason being, he had publicly supposed, that he was a postadolescent homosexual.

Known for the razor-sharpness of both his wit and his tongue, his encyclopedic mind, and his sensitive poetry — which frequently appeared in the *New York Review* under his monogram, RMS was undoubtedly the administration's biggest intellectual gun, and Franklin Tompkins, who had never actually met him before, found himself oddly enthralled, in spite of the unholy trinity of loathing he maintained for eggheads, liberals, and fags.

The two-engine Lockheed X–47, bearing the insignia of the United States Air Force, came out of a pocket in the clouds like a cigar in a metal tube. It made a no-nonsense landing and taxied to a standstill beside an American flag that snapped in the wind like a shoeshine rag. If only Tompkins could have had more notice, he might have been able to arrange for a military band to play the "Star-Spangled Banner," though he had been lucky enough, he guessed, to have found a suitably sized Old Glory on the base, and the way it was being whipped by crosscurrents of air no one could possibly detect that it only had forty-eight stars.

As two workmen rolled a mobile stairway to the exit door of the aircraft, Tompkins suddenly felt the full weight of his new priority. It had all happened so precipitously, which was Langley's way, but he had never been able to accustom himself to it. He had not even had time to take the proper security measures for a visitor of the stature of RMS, and now he glanced with a cautious squint in his eyes at Hakim Hakim and the others in the reception party to be certain there were no impostors. He saw Tahir and his aide idling on the fringes of the group, and though it was too late to do anything now, he shuddered at the thought that two men he had not yet excluded from his list of possible enemy agents would soon be almost thigh to thigh with RMS. Luckily he was armed.

A Turkish general and a senior man from the foreign ministry were to have flown in from Ankara to be on hand to greet the Americans, but the only arrival from the capital was word that they had been unavoidably detained until the following day. Though forgiveness would be begged a thousand times over, this was an intentional slight exercised by Turkish diplomacy to inform Washington that the Yankee wool had not been pulled over its eyes. One does not send RMSes to watch foreign waterworks. Whether or not Hakim Hakim was aware of Ankara's ploy — and Tompkins certainly was not — it was left to him to do the receiving, which he handled with Old World aplomb, considering that he had to convey the embarrassed pardons, and that not even Tompkins could be completely sure about the introductions.

It all went well, however. Tompkins knew a general when he saw one, and this one could only be the General Sanders on his list. The two colonels volunteered their own names, as he knew colonels always did on such occasions, and since the only other civilian to deplane from the Lockheed was definitely not RMS, Tompkins deduced that he had to be the NASA official, a certain Dr. Armstrong, and he was right.

RMS was last to disembark and there could be no mistake about him. His countenance was distinguished in its own right. He was tall, silver-templed, and as American as a pilot's jaw, and he had a smile that could sell a light-year measure of toothpaste. True, he wore his raincoat draped around his shoulders with the sleeves unfilled, and he carried a pair of doeskin gloves in one hand, and in the other, though he displayed vigor in his fifty-some-odd years, he held a hand-carved walking stick to compensate his war-hero limp. But Tompkins would not have been surprised if all that were soon to set a style back home, and despite these touches of foppishness, which he felt were to be expected from a poet, RMS still had — for Franklin Tompkins, at least — that blessed look of a man who had played marbles, drunk beer, watched football, gone to the very same church, and done only the Lord knew what else with the President of the United States.

Without further ceremony, Hakim Hakim led the Americans to a nearby building while the other Turks remained behind. Tompkins came up alongside RMS, and reminding himself not to talk too southern, he tried to engage the President's man in conversation.

"How was your flight, sir?"

"Rough."

It sounded so much like a menacing dog bark that Tompkins took fright for a moment, during which RMS picked up speed, shifted lanes, and left him behind. Once again, Tompkins's mood-and-weather theory had proved its worth.

"Faggot!" he muttered, when RMS was well up ahead.

The climbers struggled up the last hundred feet to the snow line — three weary figures scaling a sterile wasteland of iridescent lava in the bite of seemingly impenetrable ice. The sky was a sheet of gunmetal and there were clouds at their feet. They gnawed on the frigid mist, scavenging for crumbs of oxygen, and they staggered on, falling, getting up again, driven by the glacier's call.

At last they reached the snow line itself, not a line but a bog of running slush, and one by one they dropped to their knees, sinking into the wetness. Whatever had gone before and yet awaited vanished in a ringing moment of triumph, of sheer joy at having overcome the forces arrayed against them, achieving at least their penultimate goal. The object in the ice lay only 175 feet above them, and soon it would lie bare.

They reveled in the snow like boys, renewed, however briefly, by the flush of conquest.

"Hey," Tony said, grinning brightly. "Wouldn't it be funny if we got to the ark and saw a big sign on it that said 'McDonald's hamburgers'?"

"Yeah," Nick replied, "and it would be even funnier if we couldn't get a table."

They laughed uproariously. Simonian looked a little puzzled, but he laughed, too, at a private joke. Nick ran deeper into the snow. He made a snowball and tossed it at Tony. Tony made one, too, and was about to throw it, when he stopped and brushed away some of the snow, exposing a small piece of carbonized wood, a brittle splinter. Nick and Simonian came up to him and they stared at one another for a moment. Then Nick turned his head to the ice cap and the others did the same.

The bulge in the ice was unmistakable, and though the object it enclosed could not yet be discerned, the fuzzy, dark lines suggesting vertical markings were visible in the waning light. A bolt of lightning pierced the clouds, cracking like a whip over their heads. It left a trail of smoke and the smell of burned ozone. They bivouacked for the night.

The sky grumbled sullenly for hours and the overcast flickered like an old black and white movie. There was a howl of a dying beast in the wind. They moved with a drunken sluggishness, and most of their depleted energy was used for breathing. They ate a protein-rich food called pemmican, sweetened with mountaineers' "gorp" to build up their intake of calories, and they took salt tablets with their tea. It was rarely worth the effort required to speak. Simonian drifted off to find a sleeping-place. He soon began to snore, but it was more a wheezing plea for air. Nick prepared the gear they would need to climb the wall of ice tomorrow. Tony sat by the miserly warmth of the stove, turning the four sets of dogtags in his hands like worry beads.

"It don't feel cold enough for fourteen thousand feet," Nick said, casting a skyward glance. "Warm air's bad air."

Tony made no reply.

Nick, noticing the dogtags, sat beside him and spoke softly. "Think Simonian's been up here before . . . with Kelly and his 'friends,' for instance?"

"It's possible. He told me he tried five or six times, but never found a thing. When I showed him the satellite photos, he went wild."

"Strange people, these ark hunters. They got less religion than I do. Killing each other off like flies . . . Kind of makes me wonder what *you're* doing up here, kid."

Tony looked up at the ice bulge. "If it's not in there, Nick, I guess a lot of lives have been a waste."

"If it is," Nick said, taken with Tony's sincerity, "I guess mine's been a waste."

They sat quietly for a while, listening to the wailing wind. A strong gust suddenly blew against their backs, whistling as it struck the ice, and this was followed by a strange creaking sound, recalling a boat at sea. Their eyes lifted to the bulge, and they heard the creaking sound again.

Simonian heard it, too, roused from his sleep. His eyes opened wide. His face set hard against the night and he closed one hand around his gun.

The VIP group, Tompkins, and Hakim Hakim assembled in a briefing room after dinner. They stood around a three-dimensional scale model of the geothermal test zone, and Hakim Hakim spoke of some of its features. The actual briefing was scheduled for the following day, and he talked in general terms. The Americans seemed eminently bored, except RMS, who affected a whole schoolroom look and hurled questions at Hakim Hakim like a knife-throwing act, but at a certain point he moved close to Tompkins's ear and whispered, "Get rid of the Turk."

Tompkins was taken aback, particularly by the pressure on his ear lobe produced by RMS's breath. But he recovered instantly, and calling Hakim Hakim aside, he told him not to get cross-legged, but the brass was a little bushed and wanted to turn in. Somehow, the Turkish colonel got the idea, and with a perfectly inscrutable bow, meant to be just that, he took his leave. As soon as he was gone, RMS took charge.

"This room clean, Tompkins?" he said with an air of Presidential authority.

Tompkins shone. "Soundproof. Bug-free. Swept every day by me personally, sir."

RMS frowned. "Okay. Now listen." He turned to one of the officers from the Pentagon. "Colonel Thorpe . . ."

The colonel snapped open his attaché case and spread the satellite photographs of Mount Ararat across the table. Tompkins began to look at them with growing amazement, but RMS gave him only a second or two.

"There's a massive object in that ice cap, Tompkins, and we don't know what the hell it is. This is going to sound crazy to you, I'm sure, but it may even be Noah's ark."

Now it was General Sanders's turn to frown, while Tompkins stood agape. It didn't sound crazy to him at all; he'd learned that in Sunday school.

"Or something put there by the Russians," the general said. "Something ugly, young man."

That didn't sound crazy either; it sounded downright logical.

RMS smirked. "Anyway, the President of the United States

does not want this test business doing any damage up there. Like melting the cap and having the thing stick out all over the place."

"Or worse," General Sanders intervened. "Possible detonation."

Tompkins was struck dumb, smitten by the thought of the three men on the mountain — all "possibles" from the Other Side. Better level with them, he thought, but RMS sure didn't talk like your everyday queen poet; he inspired the kind of fear in Tompkins's heart reserved for great institutions.

"You understand, Tompkins," RMS went on with a deboweling claw on every word, "we have to be the first to identify the object. We have a more sophisticated payload on the launch pad at Canaveral. But we're not in a go situation yet." He glanced at Dr. Armstrong, who nodded. "We're collecting data ... So, we want absolute and *convincing* assurances from the Turks that the test won't affect the ice cap, *or* we want cancellation."

"I'm afraid the last-mentioned would be impossible, sir. This is strictly a Turkish — "

"Then what the hell are you here for?"

"I'll do what I can, of course."

"I'll put it to you another way, Tompkins. This Administration does not interfere in the internal affairs of another government. So, if anything goes wrong, we have to be able to shift the blame to some incompetent individual. Which is why we need you, Tompkins. Which is why the President is counting on you, Tompkins."

The President is counting on you, Tompkins, Tompkins thought.

General Sanders said, "This is top secret, young man. The Turks are to know nothing. Is that clear?"

Tompkins nodded. He felt as barraged as a tin duck in a shooting gallery, and he hadn't even leveled with them yet. He cleared his throat.

"Uh, gentlemen, I have, uh, reason to believe . . ." (*Reason to believe*, that was a good phrase; it showed that he, too, had been collecting data, that he was a reasoning being; now move right into it, fella, you're just a tad away from home.) "... that, uh, there are three men on the Ararat peak. Climbers — "

RMS stared bullets at him. "We know," he said. "We put them there. One of them is ours."

Tompkins's skin flushed a Turkish steambath sweat. Back home they would have said that he was as confounded as a rubber-nosed woodpecker in a petrified forest.

General Sanders said, "How did *you* find out, young man?"

"They're under surveillance, sir."

"Surveillance?" RMS shrieked. "By whom, may I ask?"

"An inspector from the Istanbul criminal police," Tompkins stammered. "He has an impeccable record."

"A dumb cop! ... Get Ankara in on this. Without giving the game away. Understand?"

Tompkins pumped his head briskly, though he definitely did not understand.

"And Tompkins ..."

"Yes, sir?"

"We have to debrief our man. We want them *first*." RMS pointed to a table across the room. "There's a phone."

Tompkins dragged himself to the telephone. The eyes of everyone in the room were on him. They felt like fired coals. He lifted the receiver wondering what he was going to say, wishing he had voted Republican.

Fifteen

A technical mountaineer proficient in ice work can climb a frozen waterfall where the holding qualities of its normally hollow ice are extremely poor, so even the almost perpendicular glacial wall that had now to be climbed presented the lesser problem — but only to the bulge. Here the surface became concave, which made tunneling into the side of the object an impossibility. The safest approach was to skirt around the bulge to a point above it, and burrow in from the top, but that required an unacceptable expenditure of time and effort, considering the imminence of the storms, and even more decisive was the fixed time of their return.

The route Nick chose, which was the only remaining option, was a straight-line ascent to the underbelly and penetration from below. This was one-third the distance of the long way, but infinitely riskier, since their tunnel, lying directly beneath the object, would be under an unknowable stress, and thus, the more they bored the greater the risk of collapse.

When, setting out before daybreak, Nick explained this to them, he believed he was merely stating the obvious. In fact, the weight load on such a tunnel would be heavier if the object were *not* above them. But Tony's understanding of how glaciers are formed made him realize that the danger they faced was probably far greater than Nick and Simonian could conceive. The compacting process of glaciation is nothing more than a monumental squeeze on crystals of snow and ice, unrelenting until they give up all the air inside them and literally turn blue, fusing with the glacier. The object encased in the bulge, itself a giant pocket of air, had to be under this kind of pressure. That it had survived being crushed indicated that its structure was somehow transmitting these forces down and around it, as an arch or a vault supports the thrust of masonry. Any disturbance to this architecture might cause not the cave-in of the tunnel alone but could make the entire bubble burst. Tony, however, saw no difference in being killed by the action of one scientific principle or another, so he said nothing to the others. Like most knowledge, it only served to increase the complexity of fear.

Nick went up chopping a zigzag pattern of toe-steps into the ice and anchoring himself with tubular, screw-type ice pitons driven eight inches into the wall. Before starting, he had made several tests on the ice and he knew he was in for a difficult time. A toe-step can often be hacked out quickly with a couple of strokes of an ax, but glacial ice is extremely brittle, and one fracturing blow can undo work already begun.

The weather remained more or less unchanged from the night before, and though the thunder and lightning had abated, the morning sky looked like the membranes of blisters. It had rained lightly while they slept, and then the temperature had dropped. They had awoken under a thin crust of ice that had glazed their sleeping bags. A hissing fog had passed through. It seemed made of chips of glass. Now it was well below freezing, and a carnivorous wind fanned it down to sub-zero. It blew in cannonball gusts that pinned Nick to the wall, rendering him incapable of movement until it passed. Even if he had not been belayed they would have held him spread-eagled in place, and with his body against the ice, the unnerving creaking sound from within screamed in his ears.

Tony and Simonian, stomping their boots and pounding their mittens, formed a support team below, sending up equipment when needed. They could hear the creaking, too, and Simonian, watching Nick and the pox on the enemy sky, grew increasingly unsettled. He continually glanced at his watch as if he were late for an appointment, but Tony knew he was calculating the speed of Nick's upward movement.

"Five whole minutes!" he announced with an anger that halted the rattle of his teeth. "Just to go one stinking step. The last time it was four. The next time it will be six. At this rate he will never reach the bulge, and we will all freeze to death. I warned you about him, Tony."

"You're just going to have to wait," Tony said offhandedly.

"The storms will not wait!" Simonian snapped. There was an ugly note of hysteria in his voice.

Nick had already been on the wall for hours. The numbness and the lethargy, the phantom whistling through the eyes of his pitons, through the eyes of the zippers on his clothing, the melt ice that somehow trickled into his waterproof parka and refroze on the hairlets of his skin, were familiar sensations that had followed him in dreams even after he had given up climbing. There were tricks you could play on yourself to outsmart cold and fatigue — like telling outrageous lies that cold was hot and that you would rest after you counted to a hundred. It was amazing how gullible you became, clinging to the top of the world. But he had almost forgotten the feeling of mind taking leave of the body, a kind of disembodiment in which you became part of the wind and you suddenly rediscovered that you had always been able to fly. You knew it was caused by the deoxygenation of the brain, but you didn't care because it didn't matter, because you'd remembered how to fly, and you began to soar just to prove it. You hovered behind yourself, keeping an eye on your body, seeing an earth-bound creature trying to stick to a wall, or sometimes it was the other way around, with the wall sticking to your body, and if you floated a giant step back you could see the whole millstone planet hanging around your neck. You knew a universe of sadness and you were happy to be free. Then you saw your body falling, sucking you with it into the vacuum of death, and sometimes you were caught by a rope, or found yourself clutching the wall, hugging scared. Sometimes you were dead.

He rested in a bright-colored hammock suspended from two anchor points on the wall. It looked like the only smile in hell. The plateau below had lost its features. Peering at it from almost three miles in the sky was like searching through water for the floor of the sea. Then he worked again. He reached the bulge in the late afternoon. The weather flung a damp rag of warm air at the mountain, and the ice melted on contact with the pitons, which were above the freezing mark, weakening his top belay.

But it was safer to stay put than to come down, and though he ached like an elephant's gout, he began to carve a ledge, on which all three of them could perch and tunnel-in. When it was large enough, he lifted himself onto it, and for the first time all day he stood level on two feet. He loosened his back muscles, and leaning on the ice, he looked into the bulge.

He could see the vertical markings more clearly than before. They seemed to form some sort of writing, tall black lines curving slightly on a grayish background, suggesting something painted on the exterior of a chamber of enormous capacity. He stared at it at length, poking gently, for no conscious reason, with the spike of his ice ax. It creaked. He shrugged and continued to dig in.

Tony and Simonian had spent most of the day trying to keep warm, and in their inactivity succeeded less than Nick. Tony, pursuing the clue that the object in the ice might be vaulted, had felt a leaden disappointment for a while. The biblical ark had a flat pitched roof, the most reasonable surface for running off the diluvial rain. But when it occurred to him that if the vessel had capsized, the overturned keel would be a letter-perfect vault, his spirits rocketed, and he wanted to shout an Einsteinian proclamation that Noah's ark was upside-down. Now, however, his highs and lows had evened out, and he knew, by the craving linings of his lungs, that only fools tried to exercise their mind at the summit of a mountain.

Simonian was asleep in a sitting position, murmuring incoherently, like a sour stomach. Tony bent close to him, listening to his mutterings, but he heard nothing intelligible, and Simonian awoke with a start, his hand moving reflexively to where he kept his gun. He looked up at the tarnished silver sky, searching for Nick.

"Coronado," he said, "where is he?"

"Where he should be."

"He goes too slow. We must help him. You do not know the storms of Ararat." He stood, cupped his hands around his mouth, and shouted upward. "Do you see anything, Coronado?"

A thunder rolled, but there was no reply.

"He won't answer," said Tony. "He's got to rest more than he works."

"He is planning a trick!" A fury rose in his eyes like a flame, then he checked himself, turning away from Tony's bewildered stare.

Tahir and Hikmet watched the briefing of the VIPs from an observation room. The inspector's elaborate curiosity had been especially aroused when he learned, by a means of communion so intricately subtle that it bordered on telepathy, that the Americans were displaying an eccentric interest in some of the most esoteric aspects of the geothermal test.

They had, for example, even wanted to know how *high* the expected geyser might spout, as if they were reporters for the *Guinness Book of World Records*, or advance men to defend Old Faithful's honor. Odder still were the inquiries that had been made about Tahir himself, and though he blamed Tompkins alone, this had gone as far as an underhanded attempt to cast suspicion not only on Hikmet and himself but also on Dobbs.

"I can't speak for you all," Tompkins had been quoted to him as having said, "but several countries, including the Other Side, have used dogs like goddamn carrier pigeons."

Knowing full well Ankara's chronic humorlessness and the traditionally high rate of expendability in the civil service, Tahir could no longer be certain that his finest efforts would escape cheap sabotage; he might even now be locked in battle for his job. Thus it was with all his attention and determination redoubled that he listened to Colonel Hakim Hakim's report to the visitors, with eyes that roamed on the latter, and Hikmet, who owed all to the Master, did the same. Dobbs was elsewhere; having nothing to lose, he was content.

The observation room overlooked the group, amphitheater-style, although it was sealed off by glass panels, with sound transmitted electronically. Below lay a highly computerized command unit resembling a space flight control center. A series of television monitors showed various views of the rig outside drilling deeper into the ground, and a corps of technicians was busily engaged in the precountdown preparations for the test.

The Americans were seated in front of Hakim Hakim, who stood by the scale-model of the area and cutaway designs of the

subsurface strata of bedrock and the underground conduits believed to contain the thermal energy sources. He had been speaking for almost an hour, but most of his presentation was only
going through the motions, since the assurances that had been
sought had already been received at a higher level. Now, he was
at the point of thanking the United States for its moral support,
which, he said, had been "unswerving," and for its financial aid,
which, he said, had been "always generous." He then asked if
there were any questions, and to everyone's surprise there was
one, because the entire session had been a formality. But RMS,
undoubtedly seeking corroboration of what he had been told by
Tompkins, asked Hakim Hakim to go over the security aspects.

"The only danger area," the colonel replied, as Tompkins,
who had been feeling ready for deep-dip baptism until now,
watched him nervously, "is the immediate test zone and on the
mountainside, but only to a certain level." Hakim Hakim pointed
to the model of the mountain, indicating the altitude of the
Kurdish village, which was thousands of feet below the ice cap.
"But there is no cause for alarm. The village will be evacuated.
The area will be completely cleared. We are taking every pre-
caution." Hakim Hakim, grabbing RMS's eyes as if they were
the lapels of his jacket, added mordantly, "You are convinced?"

"We're looking forward to your test, colonel. It ought to be
quite a show."

Tompkins sighed.

Tahir switched off the sound control in the observation room,
as everyone below stood and began to file out. He, too, was
about to leave with Hikmet, when one of the test site officers
came in to inform him that he had an emergency telephone call.
The officer lifted the receiver on an instrument panel and handed
it to the inspector. Tahir waited for him to leave, then put it to
his ear.

"Nazim Aziz Tahir," he announced. He listened for a moment,
then turned to Hikmet. "It is Ankara." They both worried.
Tahir spoke into the phone, responding repeatedly with no other
word but "yes," intonated in at least a dozen ways, one of which
expressed unmitigated delight, and finally, with a yes that was
both an absolute devotion and a reassurance of his complete
control of the situation, he hung up. "I will be Chief of Police!"

he declared to Hikmet, who suddenly stood taller. "But," Tahir went on, "I must get them. The Americans want them. But . . . Ankara wants them *first*."

Hikmet, already wearing the good news like a custom-tailored suit, tried to say something encouraging, but Tahir stopped him.

"Yes. You are right. I will get them."

Simonian was gone.

It was night. Nick had come down from the ledge, had eaten with Tony and they were preparing for sleep, when Tony noticed that Simonian was nowhere in sight. At first, they thought that he had gone off to put space between them during the night to protect his gun, but his sleeping bag was still rolled, and there was no nearby precipice from which he might have fallen. He had simply disappeared.

"He was getting jumpy," Tony said as they stood looking around them, seeing nothing, hearing only the creaking and the wind.

"There's no way back alone," said Nick.

Then they saw him, illuminated in a flash of lightning. He was on the ice cap, about fifty feet above them, trying to scale the glacier wall. Nick shouted up at him in a tranquilizing voice, the way one might call to a potential suicide on the edge of a roof.

"You won't make it, Simonian. The air's too warm. Those irons can screw out."

No answer. Simonian lifted himself slowly to a higher step. The fluorescent ropes looked like streams of traffic in a time exposure.

"Sonofabitch'll be killed!" Tony said.

"Yeah. Think of all those widows."

"Aren't you going to do something?"

"I already did. I told him he won't make it." Nick looked up at Simonian to avert Tony's reaction, but he was suddenly struck with an idea. "Sure," he said, "I'll do something."

Nick went up the toe-steps carrying three ice axes and running a new line of rope through the pitons already in place. At strategic distances, he drove the adz of the ax into the ice; he passed the shaft through the carabiner connecting link between the piton and the rope, thus preventing the anchor from unscrewing.

He began to gain on Simonian, who seemed to be losing his nerve, and soon he was directly underneath him, though he dared not go any higher, since he had left the reinforced pitons behind him.

"Got a wife up there, Simonian?" he asked, as he extended his arm and reached for Simonian's boot.

Simonian peered down between his legs. He kicked at Nick's hands with the horizontal spikes of his crampons, and continued upward. But Nick made a second stab and accomplished what he had set out to do — yank Simonian off the wall.

The Armenian, whose line depended on the top belay, plunged several feet, shrieking and spinning head first before his fall was caught. He dangled upside down about six feet from the wall, slightly below Nick's eye level.

"You bastard, Coronado! Help me!"

Nick came down one step. They were face to face, Simonian's hair hanging like a suspended mop. Nick grinned.

"You must be pretty scared. Your hair's standing on end."

"Get me down, swine!"

Nick beckoned with one hand, like man to beast. "The gun first, Simonian."

Torrential hatred spewed from Simonian's eyes. They bulged under the pressure of the blood that had rushed to his head, and his face was a scarlet bulb.

"You're in a sorry fix, Simonian. Now the reason you're swinging like Mussolini is because one of your anchors screwed out in the fall. Maybe the others'll hold you. Maybe they fucking won't. I figure, a guy your weight..."

Simonian was already withdrawing the Magnum from his jacket, and Nick had only been making idle conversation while waiting, all of it guesswork. But when he leaned out to take the gun from Simonian's outstretched hand, it was beyond his reach.

"Make him swing!" he shouted down to Tony.

Tony shifted the old rope back and forth, and Simonian began to move like a pendulum, the arc widening slowly.

"Hurry!" Simonian cried.

At last Nick was able to grab the gun. He slipped it into his harness with great satisfaction. On the next swing, he got a grip on Simonian and pulled him to the wall. He tied the new rope around his girth, feeling Simonian quiver, then he cut the old one. Simonian dropped a few more feet, righting himself, and was able to return to the wall unaided just below Nick. He came down. His face flaming with humiliation. As soon as he got out of his ropes and harness, he picked up a piton, charging Nick and screaming for his death. Nick was still undoing his own gear, but he responded by drawing the gun and stepping aside in one movement, and Simonian ran the piton into the ice.

"I'll kill you, Coronado," Simonian growled. "I swear it on my mother's grave!"

"What were you trying to do up there, Simonian?" Tony asked, coming up to him in an attempt to settle his rage.

"I could not stand the stench of Coronado!"

"Be civilized, old man," Nick said pointing the Magnum. "Or I'll have to tie a cowbell around your neck."

Only now, Tony saw that Nick had captured the gun. He stared at the hostile faces of both men and walked away.

That night, Nick slept at a snow-crackling distance from the others.

The UGA Memorandums—III

(July 18, 1977)

Mount Ararat, July 18, 1977

My dear Mr. President:

I'm taking the liberty of sending this very personal note via
the Washington-bound diplomatic pouch, and although it travels
at the taxpayer's expense, I don't think anyone minds if the
President of the United States is kept closely and speedily informed of the thoughts of one of his subordinates even in unoffi-
cial correspondence, except, perhaps, the hawkiest of hawks in
the General Accounting Office.

It may be because I write this in the awesome presence of
Mount Ararat itself, but more and more I sense that we are in
fact on the verge of the Great Discovery. We passed through
Ankara on the way here (Lord, what an awful flight through
inclement weather from the Turkish capital to Ararat — suffice
it to say that even a four-star general of the United States Air
Force took airsick), and I had the good fortune of striking up a
cordial friendship with a young Turk (hardly more than a boy)
whose rank in the Foreign Office is the approximate equivalent
of my own. Undoubtedly, Abdulkimel Haci owes his position
less to family connections, political acumen, and good looks
(although those, too) than to his prodigious intellect.

I met this remarkable young man at a dinner party given in
the capital in our honor, and seating arrangements being what
they are, it was obviously not by chance that he was seated next
to me. Thus, you can imagine my surprise and chagrin when he
casually remarked that he had heard that the President of the
United States had found Noah's Ark. Thinking, of course, that
there had been some sort of breach in security, and that Abdulkimel's thrust was a provocation, I replied with my coolest reserve (and you know how frigid that can be). It turned out,
however, that he was referring to a campaign speech you had
made in which you likened the moral deterioration under the
previous Administration as being reminiscent of the wickedness
of the last days before the Flood, that is, as it says in the Good
Book, until Noah entered the Ark (Matthew 24:38).

Much relieved, I allowed the conversation to proceed, and I learned that Abdulkimel is himself an ardent "Arkeologist" (his word). Being a devout Sunni Muslim, he accepts the Flood story as Divine Revelation, but he sees no conflict between this and modern science. According to Abdulkimel, one need only substitute the theory of a universal flood for the theory of evolution to reconcile the Lord's Word with the body of knowledge possessed by mankind, and showing a profound understanding of both theories, he averred that the same factual data that support the Evolutionists can be reinterpreted in favor of the Catastrophists.

For example, the very fossilized remains of ocean life that have been viewed by the Darwinists as their hardest evidence have also been found on Mount Ararat near the summit, and if that in itself does not indicate that the mountain was once covered with water, I can't conceive what would, especially since such fossils were recovered in sedimentary rock, which by definition is laid down on land by the seas. Moreover, Abdulkimel noted in his unflawed cultured English, there is no way to explain, without the catastrophic theory, the anthropologically documented fact that more than one hundred cultures on every continent possess a Flood tradition, most of them astoundingly similar to that of Noah.

"We are all sons of Noah," Abdulkimel said, after we had talked well into the night, "and the dispersion from the primeval Motherland, the mountains of Ararat, is nothing but the Great Diaspora of a single race of humankind. One day, the Ark will be found, and men will know they are truly brothers. They will know, too, that there really is a Creator, who judges them, who rewards righteousness and punishes evil."

You can surely envision how much restraint it required for me to withhold from my young friend that the President of the United States shares his belief and that that glorious day may be at hand. For my part, I have a deepening conviction that his words were prophetic, so much so that only a short while ago, as I sat in full view of the mountain, splendid even in the soiled robes of storm clouds that enshrouded it, I was moved to write the following lines, which I dedicate to you:

Rains of blood unspoken for
Clouds of sorrow sieved through time
Their planks were hewn of promise
Their nails were forged of hope
They carried sunlight in their cargo across
   The sea of darkness

                Yours ever,
                RMS

HANDWRITTEN NOTE BY THE PRESIDENT:

Put this in my private file and remind me to give RMS an old-fashioned chewing out when he gets back, on the following points:

1. He let himself get too carried away by the local yokels.

2. My Administration does not use the taxpayers' money to send personal letters — what the heck kind of morality is that?

3. I don't share his friend's beliefs about a single race, which goes against the code of our Founding Fathers about men being equal regardless of race, color, or creed.

4. Even if our man does find a boat up there, we don't want to jump to any conclusions too fast.

5. Millions of fine Americans believe in evolution and this Administration is not going to pull the rug out from under them suddenly — we're interested in a higher morality, not limiting the right to think freely, which would create Constitutional problems.

6. His poem is too arty-smarty. A little more plain English around here would probably do a lot more for this country than a whole mess of scientific theories. I may not know about poetry, but I know what I like, and, darn it, even I can write one better than his.

HANDWRITTEN POEM BY THE PRESIDENT:

For forty weather-awful weeks
   Noah sailed the waters wavy
Then he grounded on some mountain peaks
   Proving even God can't run a navy.

PART THREE

(July 19–20, 1977)

Within minutes of the time we reached the top, the storm broke
... I had felt that this would be the day we would find the Ark.
This feeling was strengthened by the fact that Satan was so
determined to stop us. It's not hard to imagine what I was doing
and thinking as we pitched the tent and set up camp. As soon
as time permitted, I wandered off to the edge of the Ahora Gorge,
positive that the Ark was in full view. I did not approach any
dangerous cliffs, but with binoculars searched in all directions
from a safe vantage point. Much to my disappointment, I did
not see the Ark; but the view of the Gorge from above was
magnificent.

John D. Morris, *Adventure
on Ararat* (1973)

Attacking the ice shell with my pickaxe, I could feel something
hard. When I had dug a hole one and one half feet square by
eight inches deep, I broke through a vaulted ceiling, and cleared
off as much icy dust as possible. There, immersed in water, I
saw a black piece of wood! My throat felt tight, I felt like crying
and kneeling there to thank God. After the cruelest disappointment, the greatest joy! I checked my tears of happiness to shout
to Raphael, "I've found wood!" "Hurry up and come back —
I'm cold," he answered.

Fernand Navarra, *Noah's
Ark: I Touched It* (1974)

Sixteen

Every whim and calculation, all the wishful thoughts, the schemes, and aspirations were being tried now on the cutting edge of an ice ax. In the morning, the climbers had gone up to the ledge under the bulge. They were deepening the tunnel Nick had begun the day before. Whatever it was that had come from elsewhere to rest inside the glacier above them would not rest today; there is no lasting sleep.

The elements continued to gang up like neighborhood toughs to kick them off the mountain; they were holding a war council. The wind was pushier than ever, and the sky made its ugliest faces, but the blackjacks, lead pipes, and brass knuckles of the storms were still kept behind their backs, and they seemed to be deciding on a strategy for the best time to turn them loose.

Everything, including the glacier itself, buffeted in the turbulence, and the climbers and every piece of equipment had to be individually anchored to the ice lest they be blown away. Each of them took a turn at the ax, while the others gathered hacked ice and shoved it off the ledge, the granules churning in the wind and grinding like an emery wheel on the surface of their skin.

The mood, after last night's street fight on the wall, was a sizzling fuse. Nick and Simonian snapped at each other like bear traps, and Tony, whose peacekeeping efforts only grated on both of them, wished the climb had never begun. What drove them was the absolute certainty that if their tunnel would hold they would soon be inside the infernally creaking object in the ice, and since they watched one another like concentration camp guards to be sure that no one shirked his share of the work, they knew that "soon" would be very soon.

Their tunnel was hardly more than a mouse hole, a semi-circular bore, in which a man on all fours would feel the roof on his spine. But since the arched roof required most of the labor, they worked more often lying on their backs, autome-chanic-style. It was a drudgery of worming in, chopping and clearing, then squirming and rolling over to carve out the roof, taking the ice falls smack in the face. The interior temperature was between five and ten degrees Fahrenheit, and they had learned quickly that, confined in the ice this way, they could work no more than five minutes at a time, and every minute seemed an hour. Nevertheless, by the early afternoon they had drilled deep enough for all of them to crouch in a single file inside, and, at the moment, Tony was inside placing battery-operated lanterns to light the way.

"Did you see anything, Tony?" Simonian asked when he backed outside.

He nodded once slowly, and it seemed he lacked the strength to lift his chin from his chest. "More ice."

Simonian looked away. It was Nick's turn to chop. He crawled into the tunnel sluggishly, but without complaint. They had worked on an energy reserve they had not known they possessed, though it was all but depleted now. Tony rested for a while, drinking tepid tea, listening to the laconic hacking from within, the sound of the strokes spaced wider all the time.

Simonian slid up beside him. He spoke in an enervated whisper, a rasp, as if his larynx were choked with crushed ice; yet today he seemed more durable than they. "Coronado is a terrible man, Tony. He will bring only grief for you and me. Listen to me: we must get the gun back from him."

"We? . . . And who gets to carry it, Simonian?"

"You, of course. You are the leader."

Nick came out the tunnel, covered with ice, his blood-lined eyes as gray as cobblestones. He could see they had been talking and had suddenly fallen silent. He regarded them with mistrust, but said nothing.

Routinely, Tony turned to Simonian.

"My turn?" Simonian cried. "He just went in!"

Nick stared blankly at a point unfixed in either space or time. "You're right, Simonian," he said solemnly.

Realization sank in fast. The moment of discovery had arrived. Tony lurched to his feet, stiffening in a kind of shudder that shook off all that had transpired until now. Simonian reached for an ax. Nick dug into the pile of gear and withdrew a flashlight and some probing tools. He went back inside on his hands and knees. The others followed, lumbering like predatory creatures returning to their lair.

Inside the tunnel the repetitious creaking sound was like a night screech in a tropical forest. They huddled close to one another, and what little warmth remained in their bodies, stoked by the rapier thrusts of quickened heartbeats, made the ice walls run with globules of water. Handlebars of steam flared from their nostrils. No one spoke for fear of emitting cataclysmic vibrations, and they would have had to shout over the creaking.

Nick handed the flashlight to Tony, who was immediately behind him. He continued to dig, not deeper, but upward, breaking into the ice overhead. The initial blows brought a rain of chunk ice from several sections of the roof, and though it seemed for a moment that a cave-in had begun, the fall was only particles that had been incompletely dislodged before. He chipped with a hammer and a piton, brushing the freed pieces from his upturned face, while Tony and Simonian shoveled them down the line.

Tony kept the circle of light aimed at the area of penetration, and whenever Nick cleared away the light-diffusing chiseled ice, they could all see clearly what he was driving toward. A gray panel of uncertain substance lay directly above the membrane of ice that was rapidly being demolished. Its size was indeterminate; it was curved like the belly of a whale.

Their eyes were as piercing as Nick's piton. He tapped it lightly with the side of the hammerhead. He struck glancingly at the ice, trying to remove it in sheets rather than make a hole, and when he had thinned it so that it was only a glistening skin, he began to pick at it with the point, with a dentist's touch.

Tony marveled at the care with which he worked. For an archaeologist, it was the height of barbarity to destroy the unknown, and even obstacles that had to be breeched were studied first to ascertain their nature and how they might later be re-assembled. But this was something that had to be learned, yet it was all instinctual to Nick.

At last the cover of ice shattered like safety glass, leaving a knuckle-sized hole, where the panel itself was exposed. Nick proceeded now to enlarge the opening, removing the ice sliver by sliver. He could feel the object on his gloved fingertips, but the numbness in his hands dulled any clue he might have received as to what it was made of, save a vague sensation that it was as smooth and as cold as the sheath of ice.

When the opening was bigger than his fist, he took off his right-hand glove. Sweat dripped from everyone's brow in spite of the cold. Their eyes lifted as he raised his naked hand and closed it tightly, his frigid finger bones obeying with insolent reluctance. He looked back at the others, his gaze lingering on Tony, then he turned and knocked hard on the panel.

The cavernous object responded — not with the natural thud of gopherwood, not with the flatness of encrusted pitch, or the slap of the reeds used at God's command by Noah, but with a clean ring, the resonant clang of metal forged and shaped by lesser beings come from another time.

They looked at one another. It was no longer possible to believe that what they had found was the ark, but not a sound was uttered and no trace of disappointment was betrayed, for the pitch of excitement squealed and the desire to go forward at any cost overwhelmed them. Nick continued to expand the opening. He worked feverishly, almost clumsily, baring more and more of the gray metal panel. He located a juncture where one panel was joined to another. Tony handed him the hammer and piton, and he drove the point end into the seam.

The metal was thin and the joint yielded readily, but the steady pounding shook plates of ice from the tunnel ceiling and they came down crashing all around them. Nick paused until the fear of collapse ebbed, then he began again more cautiously, but with the same effect. Falling ice accumulated rapidly on the tunnel floor, and while he continued without respite now, Tony and Simonian were kept equally busy clearing the area.

Widening the incision between the two panels, Nick was soon able to pry the opening apart with the shaft of an ice ax, creating an aperture big enough to hoist himself inside, and with barely a backward glance, he lifted himself into the object and disappeared.

Tony climbed inside, too, and Simonian, gathering the lanterns used to illuminate the tunnel, made the sign of the Cross on his chest, and followed him up.

They were in a barren, rounded enclosure, barely large enough to contain them in a standing position. The greenish walls gleamed in their torchlight with a thick coating of ice. They were obviously in only a small section of the object, and there was nothing to suggest its precise nature or size. It was like being inside a metallic tomb, or a capsule, or even a stall of the ark, but an ark made recently, and a series of machined, silvery rungs affixed to one of the walls heightened that effect. It led to an overhead hatch that apparently gave on to a higher level. Nick tried to open it, but it was frozen shut, and he began to chip the ice away with the claw of a hammer.

Their respiration was hard and loud, their breaths gunfire short. The lanterns cast hunchbacked shadows on the concave walls. Nick broke the seal of ice on the hatch. He forced it with his hands. It turned slowly, then burst inward tearing out of his grip and falling limply on a hinge. There was a slight popping sound and a rush of cloudy air poured into the chamber. It carried with it an oddly familiar odor, a sweetish smell, as if someone above them were smoking an aromatic pipe tobacco. Nick coughed and waved the smoke away. A dim, uniformly grayish light shone through.

They all looked up at the opening. Nick, standing on the lower rungs, drew the Magnum.

"You're crazy, Nick," Tony said softly. "There can't be anything alive up there."

It was the first time anyone had spoken. His voice sounded tinny, as if played through a cheap radio. They listened. The creaking was at its loudest. There seemed to be no doubt any longer that it was made by the movement of wood, and now that they were inside the object, each time it creaked, they felt their own bodies shift slightly. There was no other sound. The tobacco smell had weakened, though it lingered. Nick was as certain as he was incredulous that it was the aroma of an old

American brand called Mixture-79; it was the first tobacco he had ever smoked, when still a boy, and the recollection was mighty.

"You must not shoot, Coronado," Simonian pleaded in a whisper. "The sudden force . . . it may collapse."

Nick hesitated for a moment, then he returned the gun to his belt. He climbed the slippery rungs, entering the opened hatch, but the very instant his head passed through and his eyes took sight of the upper level, his whole body grew rigid, and he stood flatfooted on the rungs as still as bricks.

He could hear Tony asking him what he saw. He could feel someone tugging on his pants leg. But he felt himself incapable of either speech or locomotion. All he could do was think.

Holy Jesus fucking Christ! It's full of people!

"What's wrong, Nick?" Tony was saying from below. "Why don't you move, damnit?"

He moved. He went up and stood on the creaking wooden floorboards. He knew now that it *was* Mixture-79.

Tony came up next. He looked once, turned sharply to Nick, then looked again. He repeated this movement several times, until it seemed like the bedeviled tic of a madman. He was in a mindless state of shock, unable to reconcile what he saw with even his wildest notions of how far reality might be stretched. He was filled with an urge to burst into laughter, or tears, to cry out something he himself had never uttered but could remember as a child hearing his father say: *Oh, my aching back!* At last, when Simonian had climbed to the upper level, too, and had exclaimed unmitigated astonishment in Armenian, Tony simply stared straight ahead like the others, murmuring, "For the love of God . . ."

It was a B–17. The round fuselage of the World War II bomber. And the crew. Perfectly preserved in the perennially frigid environment. Their bodies, dressed in the old uniforms of the United States Army Air Corps, were exactly as they had been in the last moment of their consciousness. Eight young men trapped in a frozen time frame somewhere between the end of life and the beginning of death.

The old aircraft was partially wrecked, obviously having struck the mountain over thirty years ago. The damage was all to one side, where a wing had been torn away. Jagged folds of aluminum intruded into the cabin, but for the most part the interior was intact.

The climbers, who for a while appeared as inanimate as the crew, slowly ventured forth, wandering trancelike among the remains of the airplane. It was as if they had returned to the year 1945, the only contact with the present being the outside light of day filtering through the ice — a light that had come and gone with the ten thousand cycles of the sun that had shone upon the earth that day now long ago. The mementos and forgotten trivia of an evanescent era lay scattered around them, not eaten by rust and mildew, nor on paper yellowed and fading, but crisp and shiny and new, out of time's plundering way. Tony had not yet been born when these men, all of them now less aged than he, had pinned up glossy photographs of Marie "The Body" MacDonald, a certain Miss Betty Grable, and a whole team of Brooklyn Dodgers, who in the arrested chemistry of their brains were playing baseball this very afternoon in a lost arena called Ebbets Field.

The shards of this yesteryear had no special meaning for Tony, and almost none at all for Simonian, who quickly overcame the initial jolt and began to separate himself from the others, moving with a purpose focused in his eyes. But Nick, who was eleven or twelve years old in 1945, could recall with last week's clarity the cultural significance of the V-mail strewn across the wooden floor, the homely Norman Rockwell calendar, the copy of *Life* with FDR, a blanket on his withered legs, seated between Winston Churchill and "Uncle Joe" at Yalta, and the funny little chalk man scrawled on the side of the fuselage with his nose hanging over a wall, proclaiming, "Kilroy was here." He suddenly recollected a dead language as cryptic as Etruscan: what an "Old Goldie" was; the meaning of "LS/MFT"; that the word "snafu" was army talk for "situation-normal-all-fucked-up"; and while not all these things were in evidence now, he knew they could be found somewhere on this time-forsaken plane.

Tony could tell that not all the crew had died on the impact of collision. There were two men with ghastly head lesions thrown into grotesque attitudes where the wing had ripped through. They lay in pools of frozen bright red blood, and they had the complexion of a corpse. But the others looked very much alive, lacking only the rise and fall of respiration to complete a picture of soldiers camping in the cold. Though one man, the hardiest of all, lay on the floor in a strained position, as if he were trying to get to his feet, the remaining five were all seated more or less reclined on the two wooden benches that ran along the fuselage walls. They had died in a final, petrifying sleep, probably while waiting out the temperature-plummeting storm that had caused the crash. Their eyes were closed, their lips blue, a day's growth of stubble on their chins. They all appeared calm, with the exception of one boyish-looking private, whose eyes were squeezed shut, terror sculpted on his face. There were frozen tears on his cheeks, and he held a rolled-up *Superman* comic clutched in his hands. His name was Robinson. They all had name plates pinned to their chests. Goldberg was "smoking" a pipe. He cupped the ash-filled bowl in both hands in his lap — to keep "warm," no doubt. A green packet of Mixture-79 protruded from his breast pocket. Apparently his pipe had still been lit when he died. The smoke, with nowhere else to go, had wafted inside the cabin for thirty-two years.

Tony found a row of footlockers under a bench, the names of their owners stenciled on the outside. One of them belonged to PFC Michael J. Kelly, of Paterson, New Jersey. There were twelve footlockers, three bearing names that began with Francis, Charles, and James — Frank, Chuck, and toothless Jimmy. Tony showed them to Nick. They opened Kelly's and went through his things. They had failed to notice that Simonian was no longer in the cabin.

He had slipped into the cockpit. The captain and his copilot were seated at the controls. A long metal rod was driven through the copilot's body, but the pilot appeared unwounded, though the steering mechanism was pinned against his chest, and the instrument panel sat on his lap. The altimeter read 14,000 feet, the airspeed indicator 180 knots. The pilot's hands were tensed around the flight control wheel, his thumb pressing the red stabilizing trim button. He was a man in his early thirties. Above his shirt pocket was a name plaque reading "Cliburn." Simonian stared at him contemptuously and spat.

He rifled through the dead man's clothing until he found a single key. He attempted to go down below the cockpit through a gangway that gave on to another section of the plane, but the door was jammed, sealed with ice. A rampageous passion rose inside him as he tried to force the door without result, and the insistent pounding soon brought Nick and Tony bursting into the cockpit. They were momentarily taken aback at the sight of the two dead flyers, but Simonian shouted to them to help him, and without knowing why, they joined him with an urgency as ungovernable as his. At last it sprang open, and Simonian turned to them with fire seething in his eyes.

"Now, my frends," he thundered, "you will know why Hakob Meliq Simonian has climbed the Mother of the World."

He held up the key and waved it with a professorial flourish as if its meaning were self-evident, then he entered the gangway. Nick and Tony followed blindly, like the wagons of a train. They went down through the navigation bay, Simonian in an unchallenged pose of command. They passed the dead navigator. A pencil lay poised in his hand. Simonian went directly to another gangway, moving like someone at home. He struck a match and warmed the key, then inserted it into the lock.

"The bomb bay," he said before turning. "It was always kept locked. The B–17 carried four five-hundred-pound bombs. A terrible weapon then. Today, just a toy. Times have changed, my friends."

It clicked open after a few tries, and though the jamb was iced over, that, too, gave way under force, the door opening inward. He led them inside.

They stood in a murky darkness on a narrow catwalk that ran the length of the four-hundred-cubic-foot enclosure within the fuselage. The metallic hooks to which the bombs were attached caught what little light there was; they reached out from the wall, holding nothing. Simonian pulled a flashlight from his pocket, switched it on, and turned it to the space below them. Once again, Nick and Tony were shaken with the unexpected, as Simonian sighed with a sated lion's satisfaction. In one corner there was a pile of empty suitcases, exactly like the one in Kelly's cave, but their eyes were drawn elsewhere. Gleaming in the stiff arm of light extending from Simonian were hundreds of 100-troy-ounce trapezoidal ingots, filling the hold to the height of the catwalk — an enormous cache of gold.

"Two tons and a half," Simonian said with drunken pleasure. "The maximum payload."

He roared with abandon, reaching down and rescuing one gold bar from a generation of oblivion. He held it affectionately, then passed it to Tony, who weighed it slowly in his hands, carried into the field of its irresistible force. Then he handed it to Nick, who began to rub his fingertips lightly over its surface, distracted by the immense treasure that lay at their feet like so many vassals proffering everlasting homage to their lords.

"You must admit, my friends," Simonian said, picking up another bar, "this is better than bombs."

"My compliments, Simonian," said Nick. "I took you for a *small*-time crook."

Simonian chuckled, moving the beam of light on the length and breadth of the hoard. "The entire reserves of the German Reichsbank — what was left of it at the end of the war. I organized everything. Captain Cliburn and his men in Bavaria. The buyers in Nicosia . . ."

"That's what I call helping the Armenians," Tony said.

Simonian smiled wryly. "Captain Cliburn had only to fly to our secret airfield, which, you see, he could not even do. Make trouble, was all he was good for . . . Only the Russians knew what we had done. Many times they tried to recover it for Stalin. They hired me to help them, and I helped them to fail. When Stalin died, they stopped coming, and I could only wait. I waited thirty years, cursing every sunset, cursing Captain Cliburn. But I have been rewarded. Seven hundred and twenty-eight bars, and the value has increased considerably. Two and a half million dollars then, ten today! . . . Yes, times have changed. Now, there is more than enough . . . for all of us."

He watched Nick and Tony exchange looks that tried to measure the other's intentions, but he kept his eye on Nick. Removing the gold and bringing it down would have to be a cooperative venture to an extreme, but the extent of Tony's willingness was of small consequence to him. He needed Nick's consent — at least until he could somehow regain the upper hand, which he had no doubt he sooner or later would.

"We Armenians are a just people," he said, in words he knew deceived no one but had effect nonetheless. In his dealings with Americans, he had come to believe that if you wished to appeal to their greed you spoke in a language that did not violate their conscience, which was built on a myth of fair play. "What we labor at together, we divide together." He stared at Nick. "Equally."

"Especially when you don't have much choice," Tony said.

"But that is the law, Tony," he said, continuing to look at Nick. "Believe me."

"We believe you, Simonian," said Nick, patting the Magnum bulge in his jacket. "All *three* of us."

Simonian's eyes weighed heavily on the shape of the gun. Tony's, too.

Suddenly, there was a dull flash of light, followed by a powerful clap of thunder and a heightening of the creaking sound. All three of them grabbed the handrails of the catwalk until the jarring moment passed. Their agreement witnessed by the capriciousness of chance, they began to pack the gold.

Seventeen

They had to restore themselves before they could work again, and they passed the night in the tunnel warmed by the fire of ten million dollars worth of gold. Brawling rain and hail were kicked out of the sky by lightning bolts, though the great storms proved to be not all that great. They ran away from the lashing winds, and in the morning the sun shone through a barred window of icicles that had formed over the entrance to the tunnel.

The climbers awoke incompletely replenished. What they lacked in physical strength was nevertheless made whole by their eagerness to descend and the leverage of the brightness of day. The gold had filled twenty-nine suitcases, twenty-five (and in three instances twenty-six) bars to the case. Each weighed as much as a man. The logistics of bringing back the treasure, however, was made relatively uncomplicated by gravity's overnight turnabout from foe to friend. It was a matter of lowering from cliff to slope and hauling from slope to cliff, and so on. The first step, of course, was to send the cases over the ice ledge to the snow line, and this they began at once to do.

Nick and Tony roped the cases together in trainlike sets of five, and Simonian lowered them on a separate pulley line anchored to the ice. They seemed to have become strangers with the passage of the night. They glanced at one another like riders on a bus. They spoke only when necessary, each watching for signs of what the others might be thinking. The work proceeded briskly in this way until the last odd lot of four, when Tony, shoving it like the previous groupings so that it slid over the ice on its own momentum, failed to notice that Simonian was looking the other way, and it sailed across the ledge heading for a plunge into a bottomless crevasse. He cried out to Simonian to try to stop it, but picking up speed it went over. The rope it was tied to uncoiled at his feet and slithered like a snake. Tony pounced on the rope, holding on, but the weight of the gold, nearly seven hundred pounds, was far greater than he could support. It began to drag him across the ice. Nick seized his legs, but he, too, was pulled along behind him making tracks in the ice with his crampons as he sought purchase.

"Let it go!" he shouted.

Tony instead tightened his grip on the rope. They tobogganed toward the precipice. Simonian piled on both men with a desperate force. His own survival was at stake. The three of them together were able to arrest the fall and hoist the four cases of gold back on the ledge.

"We saved it!" Tony exuberated, as they all fell back breathing hard. "That was a hundred bars!"

Nick nodded joylessly. "You sure don't act like a rich man, Tony."

Simonian stared at him, his head nodding almost imperceptibly.

Tony looked back at the two of them. He understood the corrosive power of gold.

The climbers were framed in the lenses of Tahir's binoculars. From his watch-point on the Plain of Igdir, he could see them ant-sized at the snow line, their movement on the slushy scree hampered by what at first appeared to him as a captured herd of small animals, but chasing the unthinkable from his mind, he made a hasty reassessment.

"They are coming down," he said to Hikmet, then lowering the glasses from puzzled eyes he handed them to him for a look. "With packages."

Hikmet studied the view for a while, after which he began to stammer something to Tahir.

"You are right," Tahir intervened. "They are changing direction. They are heading for the test zone."

Cradling Nick's dog, Tahir got into his car and told Hikmet to drive him to see Colonel Hakim Hakim. They found him seated with Tompkins in the observation room that overlooked the test command unit. The test had entered the countdown stage, and the shirt-sleeved technicians below them wore their excitement on the outside.

"The test is for five-fifteen this afternoon, and it cannot be stopped, inspector," Hakim Hakim declared when Tahir had reported that the climbers were coming down. "If these people are in the danger zone at that time, they will have to take care of themselves."

Tompkins felt a bag of trouble settling on his back.

"They may be killed," said Tahir.

"They have made an illegal incursion into military territory," Hakim Hakim said. "What becomes of them before we capture them cannot possibly be my concern."

"Now hold your horses, Hakim, ol' buddy," Tompkins said, striving for the guile required by this mission. "I don't cotton to saving any possibles from the Other Side, but if they end up with their ass in a sling, *we* end up gettin' what the bear grabbed at."

"I have no horses, Mr. Tompkins, and I have no bears. I have only my orders . . . from Ankara."

"And I have *my* orders from Ankara," Tahir protested. "To get them."

Hakim Hakim made a gesture inviting Tahir to use the telephone, but the inspector knew it would be useless to call the capital. Ankara had not promised him a chiefdom for bringing in three outlaws on a mountainside. Its only interest was in getting them *first*, because of their inexplicable value to the Americans. Without this attraction they were simply police fodder, a matter that paled beside the politically significant test.

Instead of lifting the phone, Tahir merely stared despondently at the machinelike busyness below him. *Simonian*, he thought feeling Hikmet's sympathetic gaze, *always Simonian!* His eyes shifted to the digital countdown clock. It read: "Time Remaining: 7 Hours, 18 Minutes, 43 Seconds." The well-being of the climbers was now a mutual problem for the mercy of God and the United States of America.

Franklin Tompkins quietly left the room.

They were returning by the southwest route and had calculated that they would reach the tent village by four or five in the afternoon. They were making time. The terrain was like a ball-bearing field. Nuggets of lava rolled under every footfall. Each of the climbers took a turn being spilled, but the loose rock eased the movement of the cases, and sometimes greater effort had to be applied in braking.

Nothing seemed fixed to the earth. They were resting on a beetling crag when it suddenly gave way without warning. Nick and Simonian managed to leap to safety, but Tony was sucked into the clamoring rapids of a rockslide, and the last they saw of him were his hands being thrown instinctively over his head. He careened into a sloping canyon that wound around the peak. Nick and Simonian stood on the ledge waiting for the rocks to settle and the dust to blow away, and when they did, he was gone without a trace.

"Tony!" Nick cried with unusual emotion.

His voice echoed, but there was no answer. He searched, with anguish cut deeply in his face.

"He is dead," Simonian said.

Nick glared at him. His eyes were drawn involuntarily to the gold.

"He could not possibly have survived," Simonian said cautiously. "It is a tragedy . . . but our share of the spoils, Coronado, it is larger."

Nick felt a nauseating revulsion. He began to anchor a line preparing to descend. "If he's dead, Simonian," he said looking up at him, "you're right: the spoils of Ararat are indivisible."

"Where are you going?" Simonian asked, terrified by the thought of being left stranded. "I do not trust him, Coronado! You said it yourself: he does not behave like a rich man. He could be from the police!"

"Better take good care of this end of the rope," Nick said gathering his gear. "If I don't come back, you'll have to move in with Kelly."

Simonian grew abject. He sat by the rope holding it like a lifeline.

Nick was smiling as he started roping down. He looked back briefly at the helpless Armenian clinging to the line. "Y'know what you need, Simonian?" he said. "Someone to talk to." He went down rappelling to the floor of the canyon.

Simonian, sitting alone with the gold, stared into the space left empty by Nick. His teeth began to chatter.

Tony had slid about a hundred feet, riding on the back of the rock he had been standing on, as if it were a giant bird. Hugging the slope, it had carried him into the canyon in a spray of sparks as it struck other rocks, and when it hit the floor, it flung him head first into a shallow gully filled with running melt ice. He was unconscious and badly bruised, but very much alive, and before long the cold water awakened him. He felt his limbs for breaks, then he stood on shaky legs, nursing an ugly gash in his head. He stumbled trying to regain his equilibrium, and he turned in a full circle seeking orientation. Then he saw it.

A small, milky-white lake lay ahead of him. It was about a hundred yards long and covered with a sheet of ice. There were animals on the far shore, a community of six-foot, black Eurasian bears. They paced back and forth slowly and orderly, like sentinels. High above them, where two steep gradients converged like a plunging neckline on a woman's breasts, he saw Noah's ark.

It protruded from a cleavage in the glacial ice, itself overlaid with barnacles of snow. Only a snub-nosed prow or stern stuck out, and looking up at it from afar, it seemed a monolithic blue gray hulk, with the merest suggestion of a recessed, flat-roofed deck above, that, too, covered with snow. Sitting in the jaws of the glacier, behind fanglike stalactite and stalagmite icicles, it looked like a whale being ingested by a nightmarish beast.

He climbed out of the gully. He thought he heard his name being called, an amorphous, reverberating sound, as if he were being summoned by a tethering force in a dream. He ignored it, and favoring the wound in his head, he moved falteringly toward the ark, enchanted.

A narrow rim of water lay around the frozen surface of the

lake. He waded in. The water was shallow, and when he reached the ice, he was able to walk on it, though it barely held his weight and cracked like nutshells under every step.

"To — ny!"

Someone was following him. He did not look back. He was going to be the first man after the Flood to set foot on Noah's ark. He wished his father were alive.

"Goddamnyou! Come back!"

He heard his father's voice, his father's footsteps running behind him, and he could not understand why his father, of all people, wanted him to come back. A man was alone in this world.

One of the bears got onto the ice. It growled, baring a frothing snoutful of daggers at Tony. But only Nick saw it. He was thirty yards back, gaining on Tony. The bear was closer. Tony seemed oblivious to the imminent danger, advancing like a blind man toward the far shore, where the bears stood on their haunches showing anger. Nick drew the Magnum and fired at the nearest bear, but the gun failed repeatedly. Two more bears came out on the ice, spreading their foreclaws. All three closed in on Tony from different directions. Their fur was patchy and threadbare, like an old, discarded rug. He stopped. There was nowhere to go. Nick tore the silencer off the muzzle. He aimed and pulled the trigger again. One of the bears fell dead on the ice. The others howled. The sound of the gunshot ricocheted through the canyon. It slammed against the walls, screaming insanely as if it were trapped and would never find its way out. Rocks began to fall. The frozen lake cracked open like an egg. The other bears sank into the water and swam to shore, scampering into their caves. Tony stood still, drifting on a floe. He stared. An avalanche of ice and snow funneled down the two converging inclines he had been heading for. It was burying Noah's ark. He watched it disappear, bleaching in a white rage, becoming more and more indistinguishable from its surroundings until he wondered if it were just another rock.

By the time Nick reached him nothing remained, only the asymmetry of nature.

"You okay?" Nick asked, seeing the bruise on the side of Tony's head.

"Did you see it, Nick? You must have seen it. You couldn't miss it. I saw it. It was right there." He pointed to a junkyard of ice and snow between the slopes. "You saw it, didn't you? Oh, God, tell me you saw it!"

Nick did not have to ask what "it" meant. He turned away. "I wasn't looking. There was some mean fucking bears out there, you know."

Tony looked at him oddly. He had forgotten about the bears, and now the image returned to him like a memory of something he had seen long ago. "It was a dream," he said. "The ark was a lousy sonofabitching dream."

"If it's there, Tony, it's still there."

He looked at the blank white snowpile. He squinted in the glaring light. The muscles in his face tightened, accentuating all the skin creases that would deepen by time. He looked momentarily old. "For somebody else," he said, and he walked away.

"Ah, my prayers have been answered!" Simonian beamed with a paste-jewel smile as Tony came within earshot of the ledge. "You are safe!"

He had felt tension in the ropeline several minutes earlier, and had watched both of them ascend, Nick bringing up the rear. Now, he leaned into the slope, extending his arm, and Tony reached out for the needed assist, but instead, Simonian threw his arm around Tony's neck, immobilizing him, and driving the point of a piton against his throat. He drew back quickly, dragging Tony with him as a shield. Nick came over the ledge. He made a motion for his gun, but was stopped by Simonian's eyes, as he thrust the piton deeper into the flesh of Tony's neck.

"Throw it to me, Coronado, or *you* will have no one to talk to!"

Nick tossed the gun at Simonian's feet, convinced that his threat was real. Simonian hurled Tony at Nick, but when he tried to pick up the Magnum, Nick caught him in a flying tackle, and drove him to the ground. They fought for the gun, rolling and clawing in the dust, each of them knowing that one of them now had to die. But Tony, recovering his balance, kicked the weapon away from them, seizing it himself. He held it at the ready, pointing it at both of them, and when they saw this, they broke like prizefighters at the end of a round.

"It's all over," Tony said, his face gorged with blood. "There's nothing to fight about. Nothing to hate and lust for. The expedition is finished. A total failure. For all of us."

They reacted slowly, but there was no mistaking the categorical finality in his voice.

"I told you, Coronado, you fool!" Simonian shrieked at Nick. "He is from the police!"

Nick stared coldly at Tony. "He's no cop. They don't dream like him. He's just fucking mixed up . . . an amateur."

"I'm an archaeologist!" Tony flared. "And a damn good one! I was given a chance to come up here and look. On terms. Okay, I've had my look. Now I'm going to keep my half of the bargain . . . I don't know who this gold belongs to, but let's move it!"

"See what I mean, Simonian?" Nick said, smiling sardonically. "Mixed up."

RMS had been writing all morning, and only when he put his pen aside to dress for lunch was he willing to see the likes of Franklin Tompkins. The base accommodations for men of RMS's stature were modeled after the Ambassadorial Suite of the Connaught Hotel in London, and their spectacular views of Mount Ararat, in this setting of understated comfort and restrained elegance, could not fail to be inspirational to men of letters. Thus RMS's output had been prodigious, turbulent, and exhausting, and the inevitable titillations of a countdown happening had been fine herbs for his psychic stew. This explained why he had neither shaved nor combed his shoulder-length hair when he received Tompkins in his tie-dyed silken bathrobe shortly after the noon bugle blew. He was in fact in a post-creativity funk, but as he felt no need or desire to articulate his inner feelings to a couthless agent of the CIA, Tompkins thought he was drunk.

"You are staring at my hairless legs," RMS said severely when Tompkins proved unable to lift his eyes from a top-to-bottom once-over on entering the room.

Oh, and he's got the rag on, too, Tompkins thought. "Uh, I

really wasn't, sir. As a matter of fact, I was just collecting my thoughts. Something mighty important has come up, but —"

"No, you were staring at my legs, which have been hairless since September 22, 1950, from burns I received when my F–100 was shot down over Pyongyang by a North Korean MIG. Would you care to see the hideous scars I acquired in a Chinese prisoner-of-war camp?"

Tompkins knew exactly what he would do if RMS made a pass at him; he would whip his fairy ass. "I'd rather not, sir. There's a time factor involved. I have to brief you on something of extreme urgency, but you see, I must check out the room for bugs first."

RMS shrugged and picked up his manuscript, as Tompkins moved about the suite with a wrist-radio-sized MDDD, or a monitor-device-detection-device.

In the rereading, RMS felt less satisfied with his work than he had in its composition, but he attributed that to Tompkins's presence. The man was an absolute greasestain. For his part, Tompkins dwelled on RMS's reference to his war record. He himself had been too young for Korea and too old for Vietnam, and though he had served his country in the Saigon Station, he had always felt that his career had been handicapped by never having been in combat. He wondered about those "hideous scars." Concealed, they had to lie somewhere between RMS's broad shoulders and his bony knees, and they could not really be hideous if they were simply scars. He had heard about ball-crushers and other mutilating contraptions. Had the gooks cut off RMS's pecker? Tompkins was grabbed by a scrotum-tightening chill.

"I don't suppose you're interested in poetry," RMS said drily. He could not imagine why he had bothered to ask; yet he often felt something akin to a negative fascination when forced to deal with dolts and philistines.

"I don't get a chance to read as much as I'd like to, sir," Tompkins said sincerely, running his MDDD behind RMS's unfluffed pillows. On second thought, Tompkins reflected, he couldn't very well punch out the President's friend, and besides, he had a feeling that RMS was a sure-fire bet to hold a black belt in karate; he'd have to handle him with kid gloves. *Handle him?*

RMS stood in the doorway to the bedroom. "You've put your finger on the very core of what's wrong with our country, Tompkins. At last we have a Lincolnesque President with a whole-hearted commitment — I can vouch for that — to make fundamental changes for the benefit of the common man, and that very same President is served, no, encumbered with, a plethora of agencies that do not have 'a chance to read,' although heaven knows they overflow with time for bugging and unbugging and rebugging every square inch of God's universe."

There could be no exit from the bedroom unless RMS chose to move. "It's, uh, standard procedure," Tompkins stammered.

"What the hell does that mean?"

"Buggering — I mean, bugging and antibugging . . . what I'm doing now, that is." Tompkins blushed. He felt as ugly as homemade soap.

RMS smiled. Men like Tompkins were beyond redemption; perhaps that was what made them quaint. "If you're finished," he said seeing him stand motionless and mortified, "why don't we review your problem."

Problem? Oh. "Well, you see, it looks like, I mean, my information indicates that our man may be right smack in the danger zone when the thing goes off this afternoon. They're on their way down."

"Hmmm. I'm very sorry to hear you say that, Tompkins."

"Well, this cop, Tahir, made the suggestion that the test be postponed. The Turks wouldn't hear of it. They've got too much riding on the test. Naturally, I didn't tip our hand, about Noah's ark, and all that, but I thought you might want to d——"

"Know."

"Yes. Seeing that there is a chance that our man can get k——"

"Hurt. Then again, it isn't exactly a foregone conclusion, is it?"

"I wouldn't know the precise nature of the risk, sir, but I'd say it's pretty b —"

Tompkins, expecting an interruption, stopped on his own accord, but RMS remained silent, and Tompkins was left in a state of Pavlovian confusion.

"You did the right thing, Tompkins, the right thing," RMS said after a while.

"Should I —"

"Leave it to me, Tompkins. I'll take it from here." RMS smiled benevolently at Tompkins. Their encounter had given him a title that suggested both the meter and the content of an as yet unwritten poem about the Tompkinses of this world. He would call it *Negative Quaint*.

As for Tompkins, after being released from the bedroom and dismissed, he felt utterly nonplussed. There could be no outbound telecommunications by United States officials that did not involve him, since he wore all the circuit-makers around his neck. As he walked down the corridor, he slipped his hand in his shirt and fingered his necklace, secure that it was whole. Perhaps the President's friend had secret means. *The man contains multitudes!* he thought, remembering, and garbling, a line from a schoolbook Whitman. No, it was Henry Wadsworth Longfellow; Walt Whitman was a pinko.

By one o'clock, they had reached the almost level stretch of land near Kelly's cave, and at two, their altimeter showed that they had descended only thirty feet in that hour, though they had dragged the gold for a quarter of a mile. A hot wind that whistled through its teeth had dispersed every cloud over the horizon, opening the way to the west for the conquering sun. It was a hundred degrees higher than it had been the same time yesterday for the climbers, and they could almost hear, and surely feel, the expansion of blood and bone. Sweat oozed from their pores like meat going through a grinder, and as they pulled the tow lines in what felt like an evenly matched tug-of-war, the veins in their necks and foreheads strained against their skin.

"How much are they paying you for this mule work, Tony?" Nick called to him goadingly.

He made no attempt to answer. Nick and Simonian were about twenty feet ahead of him, for now it was his turn to keep a buffering distance and protect his gun.

"I'll bet it don't add up to one lousy bar," Nick went on between high-pitched grunts.

Again, he was silent. He was being paid nothing at all. He

had no money of his own, apart from his full-professor's salary, and had even had to forgo that, taking a six months' leave of absence, but when he had received the telephone call from RMS last April, the offer had been irresistible. He had flown to Washington and found the people he met there, at least those most closely associated with the new administration, a sincere and enlightened group of men and women. They had given him a scholar's freedom, and an unlimited expense fund, to conduct the expedition in any manner he saw fit, though the ground rules required that secrecy be maintained throughout. When he had formulated and submitted his plan, it had won not only instant approval but praise as well, and RMS had confided that the President himself was the most pleased of all. They had gone over the full list of dangers, RMS saying candidly that while the government could not guarantee his safety, it would do all in its power should trouble arise, and not the least objection was raised when Tony insisted on the same reassurances for the men who would go with him. He had imposed only one other condition: that he be allowed to publish without censorship or any other impediment a full account of his findings in an archaeological journal as soon as national security interests allowed, and no later than five years after the expedition. He had for the first time in his life been genuinely proud of his country when this had been accepted with surprising alacrity and a contract was duly signed. He had also drawn his will — which had given him the idea to do it all in style, the Rolls-Royce and the rich-man pose.

They had called it Operation Icepick, and though that melodramatic touch offended his scientist's sense of disinterest, he was pleased with RMS's remark that it was "a tolerable concession to the covens and atavists of the CIA" — an agency, he said off-the-record, the President wished to phase out — and he had left the United States feeling that the new Washington held the nation's future in good hands.

Now, however, in spite of disappointment and hardship, he was not dispirited, and it certainly had been a journey of discovery requiring further investigation, particularly, as far as he was concerned, of the serpent people's strange religion. And somewhere on the mountain beneath a fallen avalanche of snow and ice there was, for whatever its worth, his tortured glimpse of the shape of Noah's ark. For him, there had been much more than a pot of gold at the end of this ungodly rainbow, but he did not expect Nick, whom he truly admired, to understand that, which was why he could think of nothing to say to him anymore. Instead, he pulled his share of the load.

"Two times you rescued him from death," Simonian said to Nick after Tony failed to respond, "and he treats you like the dung of a pig!" Tony was out of hearing range, but Simonian now lowered his voice to a whisper. "We must get the gun, Coronado."

Nick was unmoved by Simonian's late bid to become his "ally." "Try it, Simonian," he said. "You can bet your ass *I* am." He looked back at Tony, watched him haul weight and eat dust, and he grinned.

Eighteen

They all had a dimly uneasy feeling of being watched. It drizzled pebbles now and then, rocks crunched, the underbrush rustled, shadows passed like the blink of an eye; but all this occurred at infrequent intervals and at distances that eluded separation from the natural sounds and movements of flora and fauna, of the wind and the mountain. The substance of these sensations was too slender to put into words, yet they accumulated on the floor of consciousness like dust swept under a rug. Uppermost in each of their minds was the unbroken thought of getting down the mountain in control of the gold.

A Sahara sun had climbed upon their backs. They were as dry as old firewood, and they had to stop repeatedly to guzzle water. It flowed into their bodies barely moistening their tongues and sieved through in a sweat that was gone before it could dampen their clothes. They had abandoned much of their gear, their backpacks, and all of their cold-weather clothing, but compared with the weight they were moving now, that counted for little, of course, and they still had to carry their irons and hundreds of feet of rope.

It was past three o'clock. They were at 6500 feet, and the same drilling sound that had accompanied them part of the way going up three days ago returned from below. It thumped like a heart as overwrought as their own. Simonian appeared near to collapse. He slowed them at every step, pausing to lean against rockface, his body sagging as if in his legs were where he kept his bones. But it was more ploy than exhaustion. They were nearing the Aghuri chasm for the final big-wall descent before passing through the village, and Simonian had reasoned that Nick would somehow make his move against Tony in that situation, where they would be totally reliant on his skills. He felt it would be easier to get the gun away from Tony than from Nick, and though, if successful, he would still have to contend with Nick, the wall, and whatever else might ensue, he would think of something when the time came, and it was simpler to think being armed. His play-acting delays therefore were improvisations aimed at gaining time to find a way to get at Tony. He believed that if he could only get his hands around Tony's neck he would wring the gun free with a reserve of bile saved up like pennies over thirty-two years for just such an eventuality; the spoils of Ararat had always been indivisible, and they belonged to *him*.

Nick, laboring side by side with Simonian, read the older man's show of weariness with precision, and he held himself prepared to act in kind. Tony paid less attention to nuance, concentrating on remaining beyond reach behind them. This he did without once being lax, displaying an exasperating tolerance for Simonian's pretended failings.

They were almost at the edge of the chasm, and had only to haul the load a few feet more before roping and lowering, when Simonian dropped to his knees, clutching his chest.

"I cannot make it, Tony," he gasped. "I am finished."

He folded like a clam, striking his head on a corner of a suitcase. Nick braced himself. Tony stared from ten or twelve feet away, concerned but nonetheless cautious. Simonian rattled a tragedian's final suffering.

"What's wrong, Simonian?" Tony asked, taking no more than a half-step toward him.

Simonian raised a limp hand beckoningly and muttered something unintelligible.

Tony made another hesitant approach, turning his ear to Simonian. He stood in the back of the chain of five cases on which Simonian lay heaving.

"What is it, Simonian?"

"*Aghrrrrrrr!*" the Armenian war-cried, shoving eight hundred and fifty pounds against Tony's legs with all the vitriol of his frustrations.

Tony went down like mowed grass. Simonian sprang at him with throttling hands, as Nick leaped, too, ready himself to seize the gun if he could from either Tony or Simonian. But Tony spun away, rolled once like the turn of a wheel, and when he righted himself lying on the ground, the Magnum was still in his hand.

"If you knew how far back I've got this trigger pulled, Simonian, you'd faint!" he said, looking up at him.

Simonian unleashed a gnashing growl. He stamped his feet and pounded his head with his fists in a tantrum. "Don't be a fool, Tony!" he pleaded with all the sourness that was curdling his soul. "The spoils belong to no one but us. We can all be rich, Tony. Rich!"

Tony got to his feet slowly, the gun still trained on Simonian. He peered into the chasm, then turned to Nick, who watched him with mocking eyes.

"This is the way we're going to do it, Nick," Tony said through heavily drawn breaths. "You're going down first. I go next. Then you're coming back up. You and Simonian lower the gold. You go down. Simonian last." He glanced at Simonian, who had slumped to a sitting position on one of the cases, propping a childishly pouting face in his hands. "Unless you want to stay . . . forever."

"I am a broken man, Tony. I will do anything you want."

"Okay," Tony said to Nick, "let's get this thing over with."

"Like the man said, professor," Nick replied through a half-smile, "anything you want." He knew how to get the gun.

The chasm was too narrow for the bowed swings of a rappel. He used the pitons he had previously placed in the wall like rungs, passing a new line through the carabiners. When he had gone down about a hundred feet or so, he stopped. He removed one of the pitons, widened the hole with the point, and replaced it loosely, so that when Tony came down he would fall.

Tony had chosen the most sensible way for the descent, and Nick could not believe that he would be so reckless as to leave Simonian free to tamper with the ropes. He imagined that Tony would bind Simonian's hands and legs before coming down, and Tony's fall would thus be caught by the top belay. Hanging in the chasm, he would either hand over the gun or Nick would let him swing until he did.

Nick, back on the lower ledge, could not see what was happening above, but his assumptions were borne out. Simonian was completely submissive, as Tony tied his hands and feet. He looked up at Tony with sad eyes, and he seemed like a convalescent, but Tony kept up his guard.

"Only *I* know how to get it out of the country, Tony," he said beseechingly, as if he were uncrating his very last hope. "It is all arranged. You can have the spoils to yourself, Tony. I want only a few bars . . ."

Tony appeared almost interested for a moment. The problem of disposing of the treasure had never crossed his mind, and though it meant nothing to him now, he suddenly realized that it had to have been well thought out. He almost felt sorry for Simonian, who continued to beg, searching for the tumblers of his captor's heart.

"For my old age, Tony. I have a family. Little children. But I do not need very much, Tony. Five . . . six bars . . ."

"You'd even settle for one, wouldn't you, Simonian?"

He shrugged. "One . . . two . . ."

"That's what I like about you, Simonian. You're so goddamn agreeable." Tony pulled on the ropes to signal Nick that he was coming down. He smiled a goodbye at Simonian, who sat hogtied and helpless, but with a fire returned to his eyes.

As soon as Tony was gone, he squirmed violently, summoning every muscle in an effort to break free of his bonds, and when that failed he wriggled on the ground toward the anchor knot.

Nick leaned into the chasm. He saw Tony coming down, a sharp silhouette on a thin slice of sky. His heart raced, living out the sickening sensation of a fall, gagging on his stomach ramming into his maw, feeling his eyes driving through the roof of his skull. When you fell twenty-five or thirty feet, the impact of the catch could crush bone, piercing internal organs, and the force applied to a rope drawn over the right angle of a rock ledge was sometimes enough to snap it. He had calculated that Tony would drop no more than eight feet, but there were no fail-safe falls, and their ropes had been weakened by now from exposure to temperature extremes.

On his own descent, Nick had anchored himself to the wall at three points, giving him that much more protection, and Tony was following his lead. The final anchoring required that he get onto the loosened piton, and his foot was hovering above it when he sensed something odd in the main anchor line. An experienced mountaineer would have recognized it as trouble; ropes can communicate emotions from one climber to another. Simonian had in fact reached the top belay, and with his wrists crossed behind his back, he was undoing the knot with a rodent's will, chewing into the rope with his thick fingers. But Tony merely returned to his objective of capturing a toehold below him, and moving down slowly, he now felt the rope slacken.

Nick watched Tony's foot probing blindly for the faulty piton, as he held the main line for support. He saw Tony pull it to take up slack, and almost immediately he knew that the rope was simply too limp to still be secured at the other end. Tony continued to be protected at two points on the wall above him, but he was going to fall, and Nick, after his gold not his blood, shied from the heightened risk.

"Freeze!" he shouted at Tony.

Tony, who had already lost the honed edge of his balance when the slackness failed to tighten, was shot through with fear at the sound of Nick's cry of danger, and he clung to the wall like paint.

Simonian had snaked his way to the rim of the ledge, and seeing Tony's sudden halt, he knew that he was in some sort of difficulty. He rolled on the ground, twisting behind a boulder as big as a Saratoga trunk, and with his back against it, his heels digging into the dirt, he began to push it toward the edge, hoping to knock Tony off the wall.

Nick entered the chasm and climbed to the level of the loose piton. He pulled the untied rope to get it out of his way. It came flying over the ledge and hung from Tony's harness like a tail. He removed the piton, cleaned the hole of rock dust, and reinserting it, he proceeded to wedge it firmly in place with bladelike chocks.

Pellets of sweat steamed off Simonian's face, as he backed the several-hundredweight boulder up to the chasm. Crimson was the color of his hatred, and it was spread across his skin in splotches. The boulder stood flush with the edge when he sidled around it to look down, praying that Tony would still be there. He saw him hugging the wall as before, his arms embracing its girth, and he sighed audibly, but he could not see that Nick, on whom his own descent depended, was directly below Tony. He swung himself behind the boulder again and pushed.

Nick, looking up, saw something slowly darkening the sky. At first he thought it was a cloud, but it was moving in short spurts, and he knew.

"Simonian!" he shouted skyward, once more jolting Tony with the urgency in his voice.

Tony, one side of his face pressed against the wall, moved only the muscles needed to turn his eyes upward, and he saw the teetering black mass above him. He tried to fuse his body with the wall.

"It's me, Simonian! Nick!"

Simonian stopped. He looked down again. Nick was leaning back from the wall waving at him.

"Let me kill him, Coronado!" His echo roared through the chasm like a runaway freight train full of wrath.

"Get away from that rock, Simonian, or I swear to fucking Christ I'll let you rot up there!"

Simonian waited for Nick's echo to fade. Then he thundered, "God curse you, Coronado! You scum of a slime!" He drew back. The boulder cast a motionless shadow on the rockface.

"Thanks," Tony said softly.

"Amateur!" Nick scoffed at him as he double-checked the piton. "You're nothing but a lousy amateur!"

The countdown clock read, "Time Remaining: 0 Hours, 37 Minutes, 42 Seconds," and the tenths-of-seconds danced a discotheque beat. The bank of television monitors, apart from the monotonous views of the pile-driving drilling, which was somewhat reminiscent of the tightest closeups in a pornographic movie, was showing underground shots of a munitions team placing the explosive charges designed to undam the reservoir of geothermal energy.

Tahir, who had been watching the climbers lower their "packages" in the Aghuri chasm, slipped into the observation room with Hikmet. He found a seat next to Colonel Hakim Hakim and whispered to him in Turkish that the climbers would definitely be in the vicinity of the village at five-fifteen. Hakim Hakim said he was sorry in Turkish, but that there was a chance they would survive. An alarm would sound at five o'clock for all personnel to take shelter. The climbers would surely hear it, and perhaps they, too, would find a place to hide. Tahir asked what exactly would happen if they did not. Hakim Hakim, who was growing increasingly uninterested in this matter, told him to use his imagination. Tahir used it and shook his head grimly. He made no mention of the "packages." He had only one thing further to say: with the aid of his binoculars, he and Hikmet had seen two women near the village riding on the back of a mule. Hakim Hakim said that was patently impossible because the village had been thoroughly evacuated twenty-four hours ago, and he hinted that Tahir had fabricated the story to stall the test — that, too, impossible, in any case. Tahir, yielding to the futility of it all, said he had no such ulterior motive, and that he and Hikmet had obviously been mistaken; it must have been two birds on a rolling stone. Hakim Hakim frowned.

Franklin Tompkins, who like Hakim Hakim was waiting for the VIP group to arrive, had been sitting two rows behind the inspector and the colonel trying to eavesdrop on their conversation. In fact, he overheard everything, but understood nothing, except the words "alarm" and "village," which were either very much the same in Turkish or had been spoken in English. From this, and his assessment of their voice tones, mood, and gestures, he had been able by a process of induction (Tompkins knew well the subtle difference between inductive and deductive reasoning) to conclude that the subject of their discussion concerned the intelligence interests of the United States. He had sat patiently, hoping that they would brief him as to precisely what they were talking about, but they had fallen silent, staring narcotically at the countdown clock. Now he had no other recourse but to adopt a tactic known in the business as "cardtabling," and he leaned over the empty row of seats between them speaking bluntly.

"What were you all yapping about in that exotic lingo of yours?" he asked, affecting a friendly smile.

"Nothing of importance, Mr. Tompkins," said Hakim Hakim. "I assure you."

"Now c'mon, Hakim. Don't play footsies with an ol' buddy. I may not be fluentissimo in Turkish, but I got a good enough handle on it to know you were talking about those possibles from the Other Side."

It was all bluff, but it worked.

"It is better to tell him," Tahir said to the colonel. "I will do it." Hakim Hakim looked away with disdain, and Tahir turned to Tompkins. "But he is right. It is insignificant."

"Now why don't you just let me be the judge of that one, inspector?"

"Of course. Well, it was all a foolish error. A trick played on my old eyes by my old field glasses. Or vice versa. You see, near the village, I saw two birds on a rolling stone, and I thought they were people. So, therefore, I was mis——"

"Now hold on a minute. Two birds on a rolling stone, huh?"

"Exactly."

"And they couldn't have been people because the village was combed cleaner than a hound's tooth yesterday, right?"

"Exactly."

"And it couldn't have been the possibles because there's three of them cookies, right?"

"Exactly."

"Yeah, Tahir, you were dead wrong."

Tahir shrugged as if to say he had told him so, and he looked down at the activity below, stifling three laughs and a sneeze.

Tompkins slumped back in his theater-type armchair. He had only been feinting, purposely deceptive and misleading, when he agreed that Tahir had erred. *Two birds on a rolling stone,* he mulled, stroking his chin. They very well might have been people, because there was a whole set of data to which only he among them had privileged access. *Two birds on a rolling stone.* He liked the way it plucked strings in his mind, like a line of poetry. If they really were people, it might mean one of two contingencies: either Our Man had somehow separated himself from the other two and was out of the danger zone, or two operatives of one kind or another had been sent to intercept the climbers and save Our Man, and both instances meant that he had been right about RMS. The President's friend *did* have secret means, and unless Tompkins had got his traces hooked up wrong, the President's friend had used them.

The brass walked in. Tompkins snapped to attention and went to greet them, racing Hakim Hakim to be first, and winning handily. His eyes were all on RMS. He wished he could give him a high-sign, to let him know that he knew, and so immoderate was that desire that it must have burned passageways through the ether, because — Tompkins was ninety-nine and forty-four one-hundredths percent sure — the Presidential Friend winked at him.

The time remaining was fifteen minutes. The drilling stopped. The images of the munitions team went gray. Outside, a siren began to bay.

Nineteen

They heard the siren faintly. They were moving the gold from the lower ledge of the chasm along a winding ridge that led to the tent village, and they stopped and listened. They knew it was the test. They had counted on it at the outset to open the unguarded route of return, and the sound of the siren, as well as the sight of the abandoned village, rather than alarming them, was reassuring. If there had been any prior doubt — in Nick's mind, at least — that they might be exposing themselves to danger, it was fully dispelled now that he knew that Tony was some sort of government agent, and anyway, when the siren faded, it was quickly forgotten.

Still, the village seemed the place where fools rush in. It was devoid of any living thing, save the flies attacking the sun-blackened mounds of goat dung that speckled the ground like worrisome moles. The hot afternoon wind churned swirls of abrading, choking dust. It drummed a forlorn tattoo on the tent skins and it sang a dirge. The crippled vegetation swayed, rotting fruit-peels twitched, empty tin cans, wearing rakish pork-pie hats, did boisterous somersaults, and flapping rags strung out to dry applauded. It was a melancholy three-ring circus of all the signs but not the substance of human habitation — until a man appeared.

He materialized slowly in an eddy of dust the way a photograph takes form in a darkroom salt bath, and when the dust unspun, the climbers lurched, Tony reaching for the Magnum in a sharp reflex of self-defense. It was Yussef, the Kurd who with his daughter Sippara had ridden and camped with them. He grinned, his black teeth etched in the sunlight. His gray brown lips looked like slugs.

Simonian glanced back at the cases of gold, then shouted something hostile at him, but the Kurd was unintimidated. He continued to smile, saying nothing.

"Ask him what he wants," Tony said to Simonian, but before he could do so another man, on horseback, was shouting a command from behind them.

They wheeled and saw him. He had a short-barreled rifle, which he held like a sidearm pointed at Tony. There was no need to translate. He was telling him to drop the Magnum. Tony turned back to Yussef. He grinned once more. Behind him now was still another man on horseback, and two more were emerging from the village. They all carried rifles held at the ready. They were dressed alike, in simple, goathair, nomad robes.

The climbers were surrounded, and when one of the horsemen raised his weapon and jabbed it through the air like a sword, Tony tossed the gun. Yussef kicked it out of reach. Simonian asked him a question in a tone that reflected the respect due him now, but he ignored it, staring dumbly, interminably, like his comrades, in a silence broken only by the wind.

"Maybe they're waiting for us to introduce ourselves," said Nick.

"They are thieves!" Simonian snarled.

Yet another rider appeared following a path being parted by the mounted men behind Yussef. They sidled their animals, lowering their heads as he passed, and Yussef moved, too, with the same show of abnegation. They all said something and he replied to each of them in a monosyllable. They called him "Shaikh."

He rode tall, his rifle slung over one shoulder in a way that it crossed his back diagonally. It was different from the others. The barrel was long and slender, like an old Winchester, and the stock was elaborately tooled in bright colors. It looked like a relic, not meant to be used, but there was a fresh magazine of ammunition top-loaded over the trigger. His face was a black mottle, the skin of uneven thicknesses, as if some parts were older than others. His eyes were a white fire issuing from single embers. The bones that formed the sockets, his brow, and his jaw were delicate prominences, like struts showing through the skin of a glider, and his long nose was as thin as a collar stay, flaring almost as wide as his horse's nostrils. He wore a hooded garment made of a fabric so black it seemed to reflect no light at all, giving it an unwrinkled, textureless appearance, and a jeweled priestly vestment with a cyclopean moonstone on his chest completed an image of a midnight sky.

The Prince of Darkness, Tony could not help thinking.

The shaikh moved his horse between Nick and Tony, and leaned over close to Simonian. Simonian looked back at him in awe, anticipating that he was being called on to be the receiver and transmitter of their fate. But the shaikh spoke in a bookish, though only lightly accented English.

"Thieves, you said? We are not thieves. You are the thieves!"

His right hand flew like a hurled stone, and he slapped Simonian stunningly across his face. His head jerked to one side, the blow making the sound of glass shattering. It left white fingers on his cheek that at once began to redden. Simonian cowered.

The shaikh turned to Nick and Tony, softening. "We are Khenani."

Nick watched for Tony's reaction, and when there was none, he asked, "The serpent people?"

Tony nodded. He had known all along, of course, and when he had seen the shaikh's carved wooden rifle stock, he had understood, from Kelly's catechism, what its symbols portrayed. It was a kind of triptych in bas-relief. On the left was a hagiofied Cain facing the east and Lucifer, the morning star; the right depicted Noah and his ark, and the centerpiece, painted in sky blues, sea greens, and gold, showed Eve in her innocent nakedness caressing the Serpent-Member between her amply sculpted thighs. The religion of the abominable conception.

"You have heard of us?" the shaikh asked Tony, seeing his affirmative response to Nick.

"Yes. A cult of devil worshippers."

The shaikh seemed ready to launch his hand again, but he restrained himself, eased back in his saddle, and smiled subtly.

"There is no devil. There is only the Son of the Morning . . . his will be done."

"We must give them money!" Simonian cried.

"Whatever you want, let me warn you," Tony said to the priest. "I'm on a secret mission for my government. If I don't come down soon, they're going to come up. *Very* soon . . . These men are my prisoners."

"They are *my* prisoners. And *you* are mine."

He turned to the rockface and shouted an echoing imperative in Kurdish. Two women on a mule came out from behind one of the boulders. One of them was ancient. Her hair was like tufts of steel wool, and she had the hanging skin of a century-old tortoise. The other was Sippara, dressed like a princess. She was furled in robes of the same inky substances as the shaikh's. Her head was hooded, and her brow and the lids of her eyes, which she kept lowered, peering straight ahead as if she were on her way to her coronation, were sprinkled with what could only have been the dust of silver. She, too, was an astroworld.

Tony stared at her, looking for her injured arm, but it was lost in the folds of her cloak. Their eyes met, bridging for a moment the immense divide between them the way arc light jumps oppositely charged electrodes. Then she cast her gaze downward, giving a quality of solemnity to her dark beauty.

The shaikh, speaking in Kurdish, asked the old woman a question. She whispered to Sippara, prodded her with an arthritic finger, and finally Sippara raised her noble head to the climbers. For another bare instant Tony's and Sippara's eyes intertwined, then she nodded once and turned away, and they both knew it was forever.

The trial was over, the indictment, testimony, and judgment read, and now only the sentence had to be handed down. The shaikh got off his horse, made one contemptuous eye-swipe at Simonian, and faced Nick and Tony.

"You have climbed Noah's mountain," he said, "the synagogue of the Superior Being. When I was in your countries, I did not profane your churches. But, unfortunately, we are accustomed to insult. We are the children born of injustice. And therefore we know how to render the higher justice."

"Is that what you were doing when you killed Hoffmann?" Tony asked.

"Money!" Simonian implored. "Give them money!"

The shaikh looked at Simonian as if he were preparing a special destiny for him, then he returned to his discourse.

"Dr. Hoffmann had begun to study with us. But he was old, stricken with madness, possessed with — how shall I say — an immovable soul. This was the cause of his death. We did not enjoy it."

"What do you 'enjoy'?" asked Nick.

The shaikh looked at Nick for a long while, examining him with canny eyes. He leaned one way, then another, to get different points of view, as if he were buying an ox or a mule. "A period of penitence," he said at last. "Instruction. Reasoning together. Prayer." He turned to Tony. "We will teach you the ways of the mountain, ways you cannot imagine. We possess uncommon knowledge. Where you required ropes to climb, you will move on horseback. What you failed to discover with your eyes, you will find with your heart."

Tony believed not a word of what he said, though they certainly appeared to travel effortlessly about the mountain. Yet he could not contain the question. "The ark?"

The shaikh smiled. He looked at Sippara, the others, then again at Tony. "Noah is with us." His subjects, or whatever they might have been, agreed. "You will come to understand that. This is what we attempted unsuccessfully with Dr. Hoffmann. But we rarely fail. Men and women sin, but the soul cannot be sullied. It is enslaved by the sinner. With the will of the Superior Being, it can be redeemed. We have many fine examples, I assure you."

"Kelly," Tony said.

"Kelly," the shaikh said unabashedly. "But not that shell of a creature your guns destroyed."

Simonian cringed. Purple blots dappled his skin.

"I hope your friends really care about you, kid," Nick said to Tony. "He's talking about a whole fucking lot of penitence."

"Yes, penitence," said the shaikh. "With a lesson." He shouted something at the four men on horseback, and before the guttural sound died on the rockface each of them had pitched lassos around the climbers, two of the ropes tightening on Simonian.

Their arms were pasted to their sides. But that was where it all ended, for a mile or so away the countdown clock laid a half dozen eggs of zeros and stopped.

The siren sounded again; somehow it seemed louder now and more insistent. It warbled on the wind, coming at them with a knife clutched in its scream. No one moved, prisoners and captors alike. They stared at one another like actors who had suddenly lost the lines of their play. A white-hot light blinked once, brighter than the sun. The wind keeled over and crumpled silently at everyone's feet for a moment of adamantine stillness, then it got up and ran the other way crashing headlong into a wall of sound. The explosion shook the mountain silly. Rocks poured; they were swallowed by cracks in the ground that opened like the jaws of animals at feeding time in the zoo. The horses reared. Trees bent down and touched their toes. A flock of pigeons caught in a crosscurrent was strung out and wagged like a puppy's tail. Suddenly it was quiet again. Everything that had been hurled into epileptic motion came to rest. Then the hissing began. The climbers and the nomads searched with their eyes for its source, turning sharply, as if they had become conscious of an onrushing train. The sound came from below, rising on a distant spout of steam. The hissing swelled and the spout thickened, and suddenly, in the tremor of another blast, the steam began to emerge like a solid marble pillar of unending length. It seemed to be rocketing from the center of the earth heading straight for the sun to link the two like barbells. The blue sky paled, taking on a cadaverous pallor. The sun flattened like a cat's eye, then vanished. The pigeons fell dead from the sky like bean bags. A dense, milky fog, driven by a cyclonic wind, came at them with all the sound and fury of stampeding buffalo, and as it swept across the slope the air temperature soared to more than two hundred degrees Fahrenheit. They were being scalded by the vapor of boiling water, cooked alive like shellfish.

The tempestuous mist was blinding; it was acid thrown in the eyes. The screams of men, women, and horses were inchoate agonies as the steam braised the inner linings of their bodies. Everyone scattered seeking shelter, groping, stumbling, pulling their clothes over their skin, jostling one another, and being kicked by the frenzied horses. They threw their riders and followed each other, galloping over bodies and the cases of gold into the Aghuri chasm and pain-releasing death.

It started to rain. Simonian, whose flesh had been seared while struggling free of the double set of ropes around him, ran into the rain open-handed, his face turned to the sky, to put out the fire on his skin. Others did the same. But the raindrops were boiling, and when they hit the rocks they sizzled and vaporized. One of them flushed the sight out of Simonian's right eye as he dropped to the ground and rolled in the hot mud for cover. But he found the Magnum.

Nick and Tony were under an overhang huddled in corners like weasels. The rain stopped abruptly. A thick cloud of vapor continued to envelop the entire area. Visibility was zero. Simonian staggered aimlessly, both eyes squeezed shut. He stumbled on a tent and felt his way inside. It was like the interior of an oven. His face was badly burned; burst bubbles of skin hung from his cheeks and his forehead like old cellophane tape. He tried to open his eyes. He could only raise one lid, and he realized he had been partially blinded. In his good eye he saw the shaikh, who had taken refuge in the tent. He was crouched froglike on the dirt floor, wilted. He made a feeble move for his rifle, but Simonian, dropping the Magnum and belching an unearthly sound, went for his neck with his swollen, flaming hands. He sealed his larynx before he could utter a sound. He throttled him until fluids oozed from every orifice of his body, and in the end, Simonian collapsed on the foul-smelling corpse.

Outside, the mist dissipated rapidly, and the sun returned to an unblemished, innocent sky. The temperature dropped. It was still a hundred degrees, but it felt like a January thaw. Nick and Tony came out from their rock alcove. They had suffered only superficial burns, but they were as limp as the stewed leaves on the trees. Everyone else was gone, except the two women and the mule. The mule was on its side, smoking like a roast, shaking in the convulsions of fiery death. The old woman lay in a heap between two boulders. She was covered by Sippara, who had apparently piled on top of her to protect her with her body and her robes. Tony ran to them. He separated them, cradling Sippara in his arms. They were both dead. He stared at Sippara's face. All her beauty was gone. What had been regal, sensuous, expressive of her body and soul, and above all, mysteriously alluring, had turned to welts. He rocked her for a while, easing her into her final sleep, murmuring, "Sonsofbitches" repeatedly, until it ran together in a mumbo jumbo witch's curse.

Nick watched him from afar, seeing an anger that could fill a lunar sea well inside him. Gently, Tony lay the dead woman to rest, and he stood and faced the valley that had sent the man-made storm. He cupped his hands around his mouth and spewed his gut in a megavoice.

"You sonsofbitches! You knew I was here!"

The sound shook the winds, but nothing else.

Nick had edged closer to him, and when Tony looked away from the deaf-mute valley, he saw him standing near, and he began to laugh. He laughed in machine gun blasts, slapping his sides and throwing back his head.

"You dumb bastard!" he bellowed at Nick through eye-tearing laughter. "You don't know nothing, absolutely guaranteed nothing! Why you're so dumb you couldn't find your way off a tennis court! You want to know how dumb you are? You're so dumb they wouldn't let you into Poland! That's how dumb *you* are! No—thing, that's what *you* know! Now, you want to know something, Mr. Nick Coronado?"

Nick stared at him queerly, wondering what manner of hysteria was afflicting him. He readied himself for anything. "Sure I wanna know something, kid. What'd you have in mind?"

"Sure he wants to know something, he says. What do I have in mind, says Mr. Dumb. Well, I'm going to tell you this, Nick Coronado, what you don't know and what you don't even know you don't know. Because only *I* know. Because only *I* know how to get that goddamn sonofabitching gold out of this goddamn sonofabitching country!"

Nick showed a trace of a smile. "I'll help you."

"Fifty-fifty. Profits and expenses."

Nick grinned. "That's mighty professional of you, Tony . . . mighty professional."

They smiled at each other now, sealing their contract, and they began to resecure the ties on the cases of gold. Tony asked if Nick thought they ought to look for Simonian. Nick said, "If he's alive, he'll be fucking looking for us."

Twenty

"**A** total success! My government will issue the following communiqué to the press." Hakim Hakim was in a Byzantine euphoria, which was about a rung above ordinary melancholy. He was speaking to the brass. They had all regrouped at the test site sporting orange-peel hard hats, and they stood around the crucible in the ground that had released the boiling hurricane like a mad scientist. A wispy, Ho Chi Minh beard of steam still grew from the hole as Hakim Hakim read from a sheet of paper. "A test conducted at the Ararat military zone at seventeen-fifteen hours today has revealed the existence of vast geothermal energy resources . . ."

RMS looked up at the mountain while the Turkish colonel motored through his script like a Sunday driver with one elbow out of the window. The slope was balder and browner now, and RMS was wan. Franklin Tompkins stood within range of his Paco Rabanne–scented aura, wondering what thoughts were roaming the prairies of his mind. Probably, he was being tortured by the suspense of whether those "two birds on the rolling stone" had gotten through. The President's friend'd be madder'n a rooster in an empty henhouse if they hadn't. Tompkins stared at the extravagant lines on his face, trying to read them like a palmist. He felt compassion; he certainly didn't envy the responsibilities a man like RMS had to shoulder. He looked grave, as sorry as gully dirt.

Hakim Hakim was coming around a bend thanking the United

States for support that dated back to war-torn Europe, when RMS took note of Tompkins's presence.

"Looks like our man may have got caught in the storm," he said *entre nous* to the resident agent.

"Don't think they got to him, huh?"

" 'They'? You didn't do something foolish, did you, Tompkins?"

"Me? I thought . . ."

"You 'thought'? What the hell does that mean?"

"Nothing, sir. It's just that I had this feeling . . . I mean, I surmised that there was a possibility that you might have sent a rescue party."

"Now that would have been a reckless and foolhardy measure, wouldn't it have, Tompkins? They'd have been trapped themselves, abandoned to heaven knows what cruel fate."

Tompkins was about to say that they could have worn some sort of spacesuit-type clothing, but he thought better of it. He knew RMS must have contemplated that, investigated it, perhaps. He himself had not even been able to dig up a decent American flag on the base, or put together a welcoming band, so where would they have found a spacesuit. RMS was one of those men who thought of everything, and Tompkins understood his anguish now.

"Poor fellow," RMS mused aloud, surveying the mulatto slope again. "I simply can't see how he could have survived."

"I sure am unhappy about that, sir."

RMS looked at him sharply, the way old librarians look at mere people. "Check it out," he said, but he was thinking that Tompkins certainly was negatively quaint.

Tahir was with the group around the steam pit waiting for Hikmet to arrive with his car. He had been watching Hakim Hakim but straining his calisthenic ears to listen to the whispered exchange between Tompkins and RMS. He had heard every word. He, too, nurtured little hope for the climbers, but if they were still alive, Ankara was going to get them first, and as the party dispersed, he moved alongside Tompkins and told him to leave it to him to "check it out."

Tompkins regarded the inspector severely. His use of the same phrase RMS had employed made him suspect that Tahir

had been monitoring their conversation. "I reckon you're talking about them possibles," he said cagily.

Tahir nodded. "From the Other Side."

Tompkins nodded. "Well," he said, nonchalantly this time,
"I don't expect you'll find any much else than a few sides of
boiled beef, but let me know what happens so's we can put the
wrappers on this case once and for all."

"Of course."

"If you want my opinion, Tahir, they were just too damn
clumsy to be from the Other Side, but if in case you lay your
mitts on any of them, remember, we get them first."

"Even sooner."

Hikmet drove up in the black Mercedes, and Tahir slipped
into the seat beside him, taking his leave of Tompkins.

"Now you watch out for birds on rolling stones, hear?"
Tompkins said laughing as they rode off.

Tahir was not unamused himself. Hikmet, too. Dobbs rode
in the back of the 450 SEL like a movie star.

Following the unpaved vehicular route to the Sardarbulak pass
between the two Ararat peaks, they reached the tent village in
a quarter of an hour, stopping by the two dead women and the
mule, it, too, lifeless now. They got out, and after examining
the mutilated bodies, they searched the settlement tent by tent.
In one of them, they found the body of a man. It was Yussef,
unscathed, but apparently he had died of heat prostration, some
sort of heart failure, Tahir supposed. In another, they came
across the dead shaikh. Tahir knew a strangled man when he
saw one. He could also tell by the nature of the bruises on the
neck that only hands as gross as Simonian's could have made
them. But Simonian, like everyone else, was gone.

He was tracking them. He had one good eye, several rounds
of ammunition, and a single passion throbbing in his heart. He
had wallowed in a shallow stream, and had packed his skin with
mud, but the flesh still burned like summer beach sand on winter
soles. He looked exhumed. His arms and his face were caked
with earth made damp by the pustular seepage from his body.
He moved in the shadows, shunning the raw solar disc with an
albino's aversion. But the sun was setting now, and Mount

Ararat blushed in a blood light; it had done too much damage
for one day. He could see them in his killer eye. He sat and
watched. They were about two hundred feet below him, lugging
the gold over the furrows of the foothills. He held the Magnum
in his right hand. He lifted it and extended his arm. He studied
his gun hand. It was steady enough, steadier when he braced it
with his left. An inner smile lay behind his mouth, for it was
too painful to move it. Mud fell from his face. He took aim.
He would kill Nick first, to give Tony a time of suffering. A
moment or two would do to send him to his own death with an
eternity of fear embedded in his soul . . . But not yet. He knew
where they were going: to the hidden car. And they were not
far away from the camouflaged cave. Let them work, he thought.
He lowered the gun and stole behind rocks to get there first.

Nick and Tony felt secure that if Simonian were following
them he would not strike until they had reached the Rolls-Royce,
and probably not before they had loaded the car with the treasure. They had searched for the Magnum, and unable to find it,
they had to assume that it was in Simonian's possession. But at
the car, they would have the Kalashnikov, though Simonian
would know that.

They arrived at the cave in the twilight. The configurations
of the mountainside were retreating behind a purple haze. The
creatures of the night were awakening, tuning their musical
instruments. Before rolling out the car, Nick and Tony assessed
the surroundings, trying to locate the most logical place where
a pursuer might lie in hiding. There was only one such site, a
hillock twenty yards away that faced the cave. It had a rampart-
like rock formation above it, an ideal sniper's lair. They listened
for a presence, but heard nothing human. Tony got out the
Kalashnikov and they pushed the Rolls into the open beside the
gold. There were blocks of lava nearby, and while Tony stood
poised with the rifle, shielded by the car, Nick piled them to
form some sort of shelter. It was all uneventful. They began to
load the Rolls, removing the rear leather seat. The rifle lay
propped against the fender protected by a screen of rock.

They worked at a weary pace. The mauve of an Ararat night
came on slowly like sweet sleep. The back of the Rolls sagged

like Midas's jeweler's balance. The silver lady on the hood stood on her tiptoes. They grew more and more apprehensive. If Simonian were out there he would let it be known very soon; he was losing his light and they were nearly done. A shot rang out.

The bullet caromed, pinging on the rocks. They dropped one of the cases of gold. It split open as they dove for cover, Tony tackling the Kalashnikov. They peered out from behind the stacked lava. Simonian was on the rampart, a black cutout against the waning luminescence of the day. The Magnum was clenched in his fist.

"It was just a warning shot, my friends," Simonian called out in words that slurred on his burn-puffed lips. "Do not misunderstand me. I am an excellent marksman. But I do not wish to be the cause of further grief."

Nick and Tony exchanged puzzled looks. Simonian was a perfect target, but when they turned back he had slipped into the shadows.

"I've got the rifle, Simonian," Tony cried.

"I know that," he said from his hiding place. "But it cannot do any of us any good. You should have used it when I showed myself, to let you know that I was whole. But I did not believe you would shoot before hearing me out, Tony. Americans play fair. Like Armenians."

"All right. We're hearing you out," said Nick.

Their dialogue had a mighty sound; it was as if they were calling to each other from the opposite ends of a stadium.

"The Kalashnikov is useless, Coronado. It cannot shoot through rock. Nor can the Magnum. But the Magnum can shoot through the boot of your car, Tony. It is a beautiful automobile, Tony."

He had them. There were two hundred gallons of gasoline in the trunk of the Rolls-Royce, and Nick and Tony lay prone in the dirt no more than ten feet away. It was a standoff. Simonian could not expose himself to the rifle anymore, but Nick and Tony were unable to move, and the darkness of night had nothing to offer either side. The moon was just getting over being full, and no one wanted to loiter in a military zone with all those millions worth of gold.

"What do you want, Simonian?" Tony asked.

"My share of the spoils, Tony. One third of the twenty-nine cases. That is all."

"Twenty-nine doesn't divide by three."

"I will take the smaller portion. My life will be shorter than both of yours — if you agree. You take the car. I am close enough to my family. We will come for it during the night. As you know we are many . . . Place the cases below me and we will part as we met: friends."

Tony glanced at Nick, who made a wait-sign with his hand.

"Guns and friends don't mix," Nick called to Simonian.

"Of course."

Simonian's gun hand came out on the background of the sky. Tony tensed his finger on the trigger of the Kalashnikov. Simonian removed the clip of bullets. He turned it this way and that like a stage magician showing the no-trick part of his trick. He tossed it about twenty feet away from him, doing the same with the gun in a different direction, so that there was about a forty-foot separation between the two elements. They were still retrievable but not easily.

"There is my faith in Americans," said Simonian. "I expect you will do as much for an old Armenian."

Nick and Tony agreed silently, and Tony went through more or less the same motions with the Kalashnikov as Simonian had with the Magnum.

Simonian moved into the open. "Now, my friends, if you will kindly put my spoils at the foot of the hill. Forgive me if I do not help you carry them. I was badly injured by the test. I am very tired. Do not worry, I will stay right here." Groaning, he sat on the ground.

Night had fallen. The bright moon looked like a hole in the fabric of the universe. Nick and Tony rose. They could see Simonian clearly. He was not going anywhere. He waved to them. He watched them move to the car to get his gold. He was going to kill Nick first, to give Tony his everlasting terror. They picked up the first case of gold, and holding it with a hand on each of its four corners, they walked toward the hill. Simonian waited until they were clear of the Rolls. He seized the rifle — the one with the long thin barrel and the brightly painted carved wooden stock. They had seen him make a sudden move and had stopped short in their tracks, still holding the gold and looking up. Now they saw fire coming toward them and they heard the shot. Nick was torn away from his end of the case, and it dropped, as he felt a rude invisible hand shove him to the ground. The fire was in the upper part of his left arm. The bullet had minced a quarter-pound of flesh, which spurted blood as black as the night.

Tony began to drag him toward a cluster of rocks, but Nick managed to get to his feet, and they both ran. Simonian had climbed on a table of stone, and standing now, he took more careful aim, going for Tony's back in the gunsight. It would be easier to kill the wounded man later. He had a moment's difficulty in squaring in on his moving target, but there would have been no chance of Tony getting to safety before he could fire another round or even two had he not heard a familiar voice cry out from very near.

"Hakob Meliq!"

Simonian locked in fear. Slowly he turned his head toward the source of the sound. Leaning leisurely against a wall of rock no more than a dozen steps away was Nazim Aziz Tahir. He held Dobbs in one hand and stroked his dog brain with the other. Hikmet stood by his side, dangling a pair of handcuffs painted yellow by the moon.

Tahir made a tsk-tsk sound and shook his head reproachfully. "That is not your rifle, Hakob Meliq. To begin with, I charge you with stealing it. Put it down, please."

Simonian stared with his open eye at Tahir's hands, busy with Dobbs, then at Hikmet who held only the cuffs and no gun. The rifle was pointed at right angles to Tahir, but the muzzle was belt level, and Simonian's finger still lay on the trigger. Simonian spun at Tahir. Two shots slammed like steel doors. Dobbs jerked apoplectically in Tahir's hands. Simonian, with a fixed expression that was one part surprise another indignation, sunk into a pile of death. Dobbs yelped and squealed and barked hackingly. Tahir cradled the dog in his arms, soothing him with the hand that held a .455 Webley automatic.

"Sonofabitch's got my dog!" Nick said clutching his wounded arm, as he and Tony gazed in wonder at the spectral figure hovering over Simonian's body. But they did not remain very long.

Tahir stood over the dead man in a mournful stoop. "I wanted to hang him," he lamented.

Hikmet gestured comfortingly, then he stammered.

"Do not say it," Tahir said silencing him with a merciful hand. "I know. He would have killed me." He handed Hikmet the Webley, casting his eyes at the empty handcuffs. "On the other hand..." He looked back at Simonian. "He was a great liar, but the worst marksman in Turkey."

The engine of the Rolls-Royce cleared its throat demanding attention. Dobbs barked at the shrinking taillights. Hikmet seemed eager to take up the pursuit.

"There is time," Tahir assured him. "And besides, I have his dog."

Dobbs fell silent, and when Tahir failed to laugh three times, he went back to barking.

The Rolls bounced onto a blighted road. Nick dressed his wound with gauze from a first-aid kit. The rear of the car was a solid block of gold, except for several loose ingots in the broken case. They knocked together like castanets, while Tony danced with the oafish steering wheel. The Rolls could do no better than fifty, the muffler scraping bottom now and then, and every pothole dive made Nick cringe, babying his arm.

"You okay?" Tony asked.

"It's gonna hurt till I know where we're going."

"Papazian's boatyard. Where else? A few miles from Greek waters. It had to be Simonian's way out."

"Too easy. Tahir's got this whole country on tape."

"Simonian knew that. He told me he could get it out of the country. He must've had a plan to outsmart him."

"He didn't do too well back there."

A pair of headlights glinted in Tony's rear view. Nick saw them in the side mirror.

"Offer him a suitcase," he said.

"Like hell I will!" said Tony. "That's bribery!"

He gunned the engine, but the Rolls failed to respond. Hikmet gained on them steadily until they came to a steep descent. Tony threw the transmission into neutral and shut off the motor. They gathered speed rapidly, the weight now aiding their forward momentum, for the Rolls hugged the road tightly. They careened around Z-turns. The tires screamed as the rear end went one way and the nose the other like a kitten chasing its tail. Inside, they swayed an old-time religion, with the fear of God and all.

"Where'd you learn to drive like that?" Nick asked, impressed by Tony's prowess at the wheel but terrified of the manic look on his face.

"Who's driving? I'm just holding on."

He grinned; since the geothermal storm he had seemed a man who had left his past behind him. Nick looked back. They were pulling away, Hikmet apparently being a less daring driver, but an upgrade was coming at them. Tony suddenly shut off the lights, and the Rolls sped onward, moving through a blind silence like a schooner on a nighttime sea. Nick was about to cry out at what he took for a fulminary madness, but Tony swerved off the road onto a rocky field, bringing the car to a painful halt. They watched the Mercedes race by and disappear.

Hikmet searched in vain for the Rolls. Tahir remained eminently undisturbed.

"There is time," he said when he understood that they had lost them. "First, we must inform the Americans."

The Tillies were giving a little cocktail party — a "collation," they called it — to celebrate geothermal energy and the departure of the brass. It was one of those almost festive occasions where everyone but the most junior of guests is searching for an opportune moment to leave. Which was why the group was gathered near the door and failed to hear Franklin Tompkins collecting data from the telephone on the far side of the room, though RMS kept a crystalline blue eye on watch.

"Yes, Tahir," Tompkins was saying eating Beluga caviar with a tablespoon. "I understand . . . Well, you can't win 'em all . . ."

Tompkins was making an admirable attempt at being inscrutable, but RMS detected something awry, and he approached Tompkins as he hung up.

"Oh, sir," Tompkins said when he saw him. "I'm deeply sorry. They're *all* dead."

"Poor bastards," said RMS. "At least our man knew the risks."

"I wonder what he found up there?"

RMS leaned his scarred body on his cane. "Only God knows."

"I think you need a drink, sir." Tompkins tried to smile subtly. "I'm buying."

"Why, that's very kind of you . . . very kind indeed, Franklin."

Tompkins felt something cataclysmic hearing his Christian name fall from RMS's lips. He blushed. But after a few drinks, it was all a slide on a doughnut.

The UGA Memorandums—IV

(July 20, 1977)

Mount Ararat, July 20, 1977

My dear Mr. President:

I agree wholeheartedly with the sentiments contained in your message about using the diplomatic pouch for private correspondence, so by the time you receive this missive you will be more informed than I am now — as I sit here in the moony shadow of this fabled mountain — about the unfortunate outcome of Operation Icepick. I wish only to remind you, should it be necessary, of the positive aspects of this great endeavor. To wit: (a) even at this late date we still have no proof to the contrary as regards our preferred hypothesis about UGA; (b) the fact that Professor McIntyre was returning with his men so soon after the ascent suggests a certain urgency that is consistent only with that very hypothesis, for if he had found nothing, surely he would not have been on his way back so prematurely, and if, on the other hand, he had discovered something of an advanced technological nature, he certainly would have remained at the UGA site much longer than he did, if only because of the infinitely greater complexity of such a find as compared with the relative simplicity of the biblical vessel.

Thus, while an "educated guess" would have to place the emphasis on the latter of the two words, it seems to me that one would not be entirely unreasonable in surmising that the good professor was in fact hieing home to report (in a preliminary fashion, to be sure) that UGA *is* Noah's Ark. Of course, only future research can confirm such a supposition, but as a result of the young scholar's valorous expedition, we have, I believe, taken a giant step along the tortuous (and already grief-laden) road of discovery.

It is for this reason that I desire to recommend without reservation that you take into consideration the posthumous conferral of the Presidential Medal of Freedom on Professor McIntyre for heroism in conducting operations in behalf of the national security of the United States. I know you will recognize immediately the significance such a noble gesture on your part will have when at some future date history records this proud and ongoing chapter in your Administration.

Now, I should like to speak to you of an entirely unrelated matter concerning the resident CIA agent here, with whom [SEGMENT HAND-OBLITERATED WITH A HEAVY FELT PEN BY THE PRESIDENT.]

Yours ever,
RMS

HANDWRITTEN NOTE BY THE PRESIDENT: This is perfect hogwash! I don't want to hear any more about Ararat until we find out for sure what the dickens is up there! With the world situation steadily going to rot, we can't be wasting one cent more of the American people's time and money on Bible stories than is absolutely necessary! Remind me to reassign RMS. If he likes the mountain air so much, let's make him ambassador to Outer Mongolia. Okay on the medal for McIntyre, though, but I want the thing redesigned first. It's little touches that count big (JFK told me that). I've got my own design ideas, and from now on I want them made out of gold — each and every one of them a whole ounce (which will help keep the price down). Also, get me a new Magic Marker.

PART FOUR

(July 21, 1977—?)

There is a special lesson for each of us in the story of Noah and the Ark. All we have to do is find it for ourselves and apply it!

Dave Balsiger and Charles E. Sellier, Jr.,
In Search of Noah's Ark (1976)

Twenty-one

The dawning sun rolled back the cover of night clouds like a can of sardines. A regiment of first light advanced across the Plain of Igdir wearing solid pinks. Frail shadows ran way out west with neither plan nor purpose, then slowly started back again. The new day made a house call at the cave where Nick and Tony had parked the Rolls to pass the night. It brought vitamin-D and bad news.

They were asleep in the front seats, and when the alarm of the sunrise clock went off, Tony awakened first. A long shadow lay on the hood and windshield of the car. Tony bolted as he looked up at the entrance to the cave, stirring Nick to conscious life.

Nick said, "Holy . . . fucking . . . shit."

Strung on mountaineering ropes anchored somewhere outside and above them, and hanging upside down like a butchered pig, was the bloated body of Simonian, leaking blood.

Tony's hand shot out for the ignition key. He started the engine, shoved the gearstick low, and stepped on the accelerator the way one might kill a black widow. The tires spun and howled, gripped ground, and the Rolls charged the hanging corpse blocking its way. It slammed. Bones cracked. Limbs beat against the windshield, shattering it. Simonian's head went under the rear wheel. They could feel the squash beneath the weight of the gold as the car broke into the clear, dripping human mash.

The four armed horsemen who had been with the shaikh leaped to their mounts. The Rolls bucked on the uneven terrain, no match for the horses, here, and the open road lay an unhealthy distance away. One of the horsemen fired. The bullet stung a fender. Nick, opening the window and taking the Kalashnikov in his one good arm, said something to Tony about having enough gasoline in the trunk to start a small Arab country. Tony's hands were fighting the rattling steering wheel. He didn't answer, but he worried as much as Nick. Another bullet hit the side of the trunk ripping away a taillight. Nick got off a shot that struck one of the horses, the rider catapulting into the air. Another horseman came up alongside the car on Tony's side. Tony swerved, ramming the horse's legs, and the man was thrown, sliding over the roof of the Rolls. Nick fired again at one of the remaining two riders. He missed. Tony brought the car onto the road. He picked up some speed, but not much. One of the riders who had been thrown fired a bullet that pierced the rear window. It buried itself in the gold. The two mounted men continued the pursuit on the road. The Rolls gained slowly, Nick exchanging wasted bullets with the horsemen. They suddenly drew their mounts to a halt. They could no longer overtake the car, but their aim would improve from a standing position. They fired at the tires. The sheet of steel that formed the lid of the trunk tore open, rising like a shark fin. The Rolls disappeared around a bend.

Nick looked back. The car was half a ruin, but they had won the race. He set the rifle between his legs, leaned into the upholstery, and heaved a sigh of relief. Tony, too.

"Whose car is this, anyway?" Nick asked.

"Well, I bought it, that is, the CIA bought it from a used-car dealer in Monaco. But I'll give you one guess whose it was."

"His?"

Tony shook no, then smiled. "Hers."

They crossed all of Turkey that day and the next. A tire went flat, the radiator boiled over, they had to buy a new battery, which turned out to be a great event for the local populace, and at different times both Nick and Tony got the runs, but nothing

else went amiss. They did see a light plane overhead more than
once.

Papazian's boatyard and the whole village of Cesme lay plas-
tered in a cold night mist. Foghorns mooed, but the visibility, or
lack of it, was a more compelling admonition; the waters of
the Aegean were fit only for Russian roulette of the sea.

Aram Papazian came out of his shack when he heard an approaching car. He had been expecting his cousin all day. The
suspense had been frazzling, and chasing his most worrisome
thoughts from mind, he had happily given him up as fogged in
for the night. Tomorrow morning would be soon enough. Now,
however, as the blur of headlights nodded yes on the road
bumps, he ran to greet his cousin, coming face to face with the
men about whom he had made covenants with God to be faith-
fully fulfilled if only they were dead.

Nick and Tony got out of the battered Rolls. Papazian shrank
like a puddle in the sun.

"Simonian didn't make it," Tony said. "We go ahead as
planned."

Papazian, regarding them with a stray dog's temerity, glanced
at Nick's bandaged arm. Nick handed him a bar of gold and
opened the rear door of the Rolls. Awe-struck, Papazian took
the ingot and leaned inside the car. He drew a cupful of mist
into his lungs as he gasped.

"The fog," he said to his new associates, "we must . . ."

Tony made a four-star general's gesture for him to carry on,
and Papazian, returning the gold bar to Nick, began at once to
unload. They watched him for a while, listening to a distant
accordion making cacophonic music somewhere in the village.

Tahir sat near the door in a corner of Cesme's most popular
café, feeding cubes of lamb run through with a skewer to Dobbs.
The bar was doing holiday business, packed with Turkish seamen, shore-bound by the fog. They were a rowdy bunch, paying
scarce attention to the accordionist, and when he broke into
"Red Sails in the Sunset," only Tahir hummed along, the lyrics
making pirouettes in his mind. He was just getting to the part

about someone's love being carried home safely, when Hikmet
rushed in so replete with uncustomary excitement that he forgot
to close the front door, and a whole gang of barrel-chested Greek
fog began to follow him in. In his state, Hikmet had no chance
whatsoever to get a word out, though he tried athletically.

"I know," Tahir said calming him. "They are here ... but,
there is time ..."

More than a few of the seamen were shouting at Hikmet to
close the door, but Tahir had not yet completed his thought. He
extended his hand and showed Hikmet the fog, as if he were
introducing an old friend.

"I ask you," he said. "Where can they go in this ... yoghurt?"

A sailor with a belligerent gait and cannons for arms was
shuffling toward Hikmet, reminding him about the door. Tahir,
offering Dobbs more kebab, nodded to Hikmet to close it. He
obeyed, of course, but the seafaring bully demanded an apology,
too, and since Hikmet felt socks in his throat, it was left to Tahir
to comply. He did so with grace and humility, showing the fine
mettle of Ankara's candidate for Istanbul's future top cop.

In the morning, the sun rolled up its sleeves and went to work
on the fog, raising it like a bathroom window. By eight o'clock
the old launch that Simonian, in the summertime of his fondest
dreams, had renamed *Oskedar* was ready to sail. The foghorns
still advised against it, but little doubt remained that within an
hour or two it would be a splendid day.

Nick and Tony, eager to be on their way but looking as pleased
as jack-o'-lanterns, were already aboard, and Papazian was dock-
side casting off. The engine gurgled. The deck was covered port
to starboard with the suitcases. The faithful Rolls-Royce, now
crippled and moribund, stood at water's edge, and if it had been
possible, it would have been wishing them, with a lump in every
cylinder, farewell and Godspeed.

Papazian untied the last rope, jumped on the boat, and hauled
anchor. He checked the pressure gauges of the engine and shook
his head unhappily, but not more so. Far more unsettling for
all of them was the wowing of the sirens. A locust colony of
police cars and trucks suddenly darkened the entire area. Hel-
meted men poured out of vehicles like coal from a scuttle, bear-

ing enough armor and weaponry to take nearby Izmir, where they had in fact come from, leaving a serious power vacuum in the city. Carrying see-through, bullet-proof shields, they began to line up in attack formation, but before any shots were fired, a police official shouted a demand that the *Oskedar* surrender.

Papazian, were the stakes not so high, surely would have acquiesced but he needed no prompting from the others now, and he throttled the engine full speed ahead, which, however, had only minimal effect. The officer gave the order to open fire and charge.

Tahir sat in the back of an unmarked car with Hikmet and Dobbs. He had every reason to anticipate a bloodless victory, and even when the shooting began, he did not expect it to last very long.

"Chief of Police," he murmured to himself, trying it on for size.

The *Oskedar* began to move, inching away from the dock. Some of the Turks tried to leap aboard, but Nick and Tony fought them off, forcing them back into the water. Papazian, at the wheel, was the main target, and before very long he was hit by a barrage of gunfire that toppled him overboard in a St. Vitus' dance of death. Nick took the controls. Amid shouts from the commander, there was a sudden pause in the onslaught, and when Nick looked up for a moment, he saw the police rapidly assembling a heavy duty bazooka. They were going to sink the *Oskedar*. The launch chugged forward, and what it lacked in velocity it made up for in noise. Tony got out the Kalashnikov. Nick saw him taking careful aim, but what he could do against a 3.5-inch bazooka seemed questionable. The police fired their first, range-finding shell. It fell short of the boat but sent up a tower of water, drenching Nick and Tony. Tony reaimed and fired. The bullet struck the mark: the trunk of the Rolls-Royce. Princess Grace's old Silver Shadow exploded, destroying the bazooka and scattering the gunners. The Rolls, loyal to the last, glowed in a glorious ball of flame, erecting an unbreachable wall of heat that drove the police in full retreat.

"A beautiful automobile!" Tony cried doing a Simonian accent.

Nick was smiling as the engine of the *Oskedar* widened the

distance from ship to shore. The defeated Izmir garrison could do no better than stand and watch through their shields to protect them from the heat.

Tahir, for the first time as far as Hikmet could recall, lost his self-control. He snapped an order at the driver, using a profanity, and as the car pulled away, he avoided Hikmet's eyes. Dobbs's too. But they had not gone more than fifty yards when his composure returned, and he looked at Hikmet and smiled.

"There is still time."

It was his use of the word "still" that troubled Hikmet.

The *Oskedar* was doing eight gorgeous knots. The sun had swallowed the fog and the Aegean sparkled green from top to bottom. The island of Chios, known for *mastikha*, hospitality, and lack of Turkish jurisdiction, lay on the horizon. Nick and Tony looked out at the island. A salty breeze ruffled their hair. The sea was as calm as a glass of *mastikha*, as calming, too. The boat rocked like a cradle. Birds, Greek birds, were flying their way to receive them. It was most unlikely, but they thought they heard someone plucking a bozouiki. Tony studied the mountainous profile of Chios.

"You know," he said, "the Greeks believed the ark landed on Mount Parnassus."

Nick looked at him as if he were mad.

Tony smiled. "Shows you how wrong you can be."

"I'm sure gonna miss my dog," Nick said. He shook his head a little sadly, and looking down, he saw water seeping into the *Oskedar*. "Hey, this tub's leaking!"

Tony shrugged. "We'll reach the island before —"

The sound of another craft interrupted him. A Coast Guard cutter was racing toward them flying the Turkish crescent. It overtook them in a matter of seconds. Sailors, carrying submachine guns, stood on deck. An officer raised an electronic megaphone. Tahir stood next to him effervescing jubilation. Hikmet was poker-faced. Nick and Tony looked scared. The officer hailed them.

"In the name of the Turkish government, I order you to stop!"

The sailors, poised to fire, implied that he meant what he had said. Nick shut the engine. The cutter drew alongside the launch. The sailors rolled a small gangplank over ball-bearing wheels and bridged the two vessels. Hikmet handed Dobbs to Tahir. Tahir boarded the *Oskedar*. The officer, Hikmet, and the armed sailors followed.

"You forgot something, Mr. Coronado," Tahir said smiling.

Nick, delighted to see his dog, sent out welcoming arms, and Dobbs barked and wriggled excitedly trying to jump to his master, but Tahir held him firmly. The sailors relieved Tony of his rifle. Another Coast Guard cutter was approaching but no one paid it much mind, as Tahir, still holding Dobbs and standing among the suitcases, took another step toward Nick. The inspector had the eyes of a triumphant admiral about to dictate the terms of surrender to an enemy navy.

"So, Mr. Coronado, just like in a Humphrey Bogart movie, we meet again."

"I never saw that one."

Tahir laughed in triplicate, and perceiving that Nick expected a sneeze, which did not materialize, he breathed deeply, and said, "Ah, the sea air. It is good for a sorry nose like me."

"What can we do for you, Tahir?"

"I am here to make fair exchanges, Mr. Coronado. *You* will come with me to Ankara, and *I* will go with you to Ankara." Laugh, laugh, laugh. "*I* will give you this," he said, releasing Dobbs, who leaped into Nick's arms and began licking his face joyously, "and *you* . . ." He reached for one of the suitcases. ". . . will give me *this!*"

The suitcase flew in his hands as if it had decided to jump overboard, for he had miscalculated its weight. In fact it was empty. He shook it like a bad boy, then threw it down and lifted another. It, too, was empty. He motioned to Hikmet, who began to open the suitcases, finding every one of them as empty as last year's birds' nests.

While Tahir stared at Nick and Tony, fuming, the second Coast Guard cutter drew up along the side of the *Oskedar*. Another bridge was rolled out and another officer with armed sailors boarded. Their uniforms were different from those of the Turks. The second cutter was flying the Greek flag. The Greek officer and the Turkish officer, standing astern, engaged themselves in a heated discussion, as Tahir, giving them none of his attention, ordered the Turkish sailors to thoroughly search the boat. Tahir, in sharp contrast to Nick and Tony, and especially Dobbs, grew decidedly uneasy and he himself began to look around. The argument between the officers continued in a chauvinistic mixture of Greek and Turkish. The Turkish sailors completed their search, reporting to Tahir. Nothing. Zero. Not even enough to make a single Presidential Medal of Freedom.

Tahir was as angry as Rumpelstilskin. "You will come back with us!" he shouted at Nick, Tony, and Dobbs.

Nick looked at the Greek and Turkish officers, who appeared to have arrived at some conclusion, turning away from each other like warriors having had their say at a truce.

"I don't think so," said Nick.

Rolling a string of worry beads in his hands, the Greek officer stood back to back with his Turkish counterpart, who broke the symmetry, coming up to Tahir. He whispered something to him. Tahir was stunned, crestfallen, but he quickly caught hold of himself, recapturing his old smile, or at least the better part of it — which was the most he would ever regain for the rest of cosmic time

"It seems we are in Greek waters, Mr. Coronado . . ."

Nick shrugged.

Tahir studied him for a while. His eyes were drawn downward. He saw the water seeping into the boat, and looked up at Nick, still smiling. "Be careful, Mr. Coronado . . ." He splashed the seepage lightly with his toe. "Or, can you also walk on water?"

"No," said Nick, nodding to Tony, "but my friend can."

Tahir laughed three times, then spoke to Nick man to man. "Now you can tell me. Where is it?"

Nick took him around the shoulders and walked with him, leading him out of hearing range of everyone else, and at the same time he eased him toward the gangplank to the Turkish boat.

"It's the oldest trick in the book, Tahir," he said softly. "You swallow it . . . and get it all back in the morning."

Tahir smiled sourly. He nodded his head once or twice, and began to cross the bridge, but he suddenly whipped around pointing a mean finger at Nick.

"I will get you!"

Tahir boarded the cutter. Hikmet and the other Turks followed, funeral-procession style. They drew in the bridge. They sailed.

The Greek captain, in the fullest elation of his great victory for the cause of international law, beamed it all on Nick and Tony.

"Welcome to Greece!" he exclaimed as if he were the owner of a brand-new restaurant. "Can we be of service?"

"Well," said Tony, "we're taking on water."

The officer waved a friendly hand that said they need not give the matter a second thought. He hawked a few commands at his crew and they busied themselves at once fixing a tow line between their cutter and the leaky *Oskedar*.

Nazim Aziz Tahir stood aft watching the launch being hauled to safety by the Greek Coast Guard. He was curled, his hands driven deeply into his pockets, his shoulders hunched around him like a cape, as if to warm his broken heart. He bore no lasting malice for Nick and Tony, and he was already feeling a romantic emptiness, having bade his farewell to Dobbs. Yet, as he clenched his fists until he shook from head to toe, he sagged with granite hatred for Simonian, less for having thwarted his highest ambition once again than for befooling him with some sort of prestidigitating party trick — and all this, so to speak, from the grave. Hikmet was beside him, but he was not very comforting, for the inspector was being tossed by the riptide of the young detective's brain waves.

"You are right!" Tahir raged. "I should have got them before!"

Hikmet did not deny it. Tahir returned to his westward view, observing the lost field of battle with Napoleonic intensity. The *Oskedar* seemed perilously low on the seascape, as if it were half full of water, and recalling the puddle of seepage he had splashed with his toe, two trite little proverbs occurred to him in such rapid succession that they were fused together in an atomic light in his mind. He thought, *One mole does not a mountain make!*

"I know where it is!" he cried out, as though he had been

clobbered by Newton's apple. He grabbed Hikmet by his lapels.
"I know where it is!"

Hikmet wondered if there were any sedatives on board.

Tahir lost interest in him and bellowed at Nick and Tony, who
could not possibly hear him.

"I KNOW WHERE IT IS!"

They could see him, however: a crapulently gesticulating Mr.
Peanut receding toward the horizon. Had he forgotten to stamp
their passports? Did he have a message for his brother in Connekticut?"

"You know something?" said Nick. "I think he knows where
it fucking is."

They grinned to their wisdom teeth. They waved back to
him in their own fashion. Nick slapped the crook of his raised
right arm, Tony jabbed his middle finger at the sky, and Dobbs
made lots of movements with his head as he barked three times
and sneezed.

O, a happier threesome was never seen in Greece, the Greek
captain thought in Greek, recalling a line from his Euripides.
He was leaning over the rail of his cutter studying them and the
low-slung launch from behind, and he found something inex-
plicably odd in every direction. There were quirks in his de-
meanor that remotely resembled Tahir's, though Nick and Tony,
divinely transported between the thighs of joy, failed to notice.
Perhaps it was in the way he was thinking, slowly wearing down
his worry beads. He was even worrying. About what, however,
in this particular moment he was most unsure. Thinking and
worrying — so much so that in a brief distraction he dropped
the beads in the sea.

They sank in the limpid water and came to rest on the Aegean
floor, looking up like a hundred pearly eyes; looking up at ten
million dollars in very negotiable bars of gold gliding through
the green. Seven hundred and twenty-eight ingots, ensnared
like a fisherman's proudest catch in a dozen nets, and suspended
from the keel of the *Oskedar*.*

---

* *Oskedar:* an Armenian word meaning "Golden Age."

A Letter to the President of the United States of America from the Author

(October 3, 1977)

My dear Mr. President:

At the suggestion of the Special Assistant to the President for Constitutional Affairs, I herewith respectfully submit an identical copy of my manuscript entitled *The Spoils of Ararat*, dispatched today to my publishers.

I can only imagine how busy you must be, sir, but I earnestly hope you find the time to read it, and if you do, it seems to me that it may not be unlikely that some questions will arise in your mind. For example: Who leaked the UGA Memorandums? Where are Nick and Tony? What happened to the gold? Where is Dobbs? Et cetera.

I believe it is reasonably clear from the internal evidence of this book that perhaps I alone am in a position to provide such answers. With all due respect for the Highest Office in the Land, however, I cannot, in good conscience, abrogate a covenant of secrecy undertaken between myself and my informants, and as I and my attorneys have advised the Presidential Assistant for Constitutional Affairs, I must therefore invoke my rights as a United States citizen under the First and Fifth Amendments. On the other hand, I feel it is my *duty* as a citizen to volunteer as much information as I possibly can insofar as it concerns the national security of the United States.

Thus, it may not be entirely insignificant if I were to mention that I was able to gain access to the UGA Memorandums through someone in Washington, who from the outset of our encounters asked that he be known only as Mr. Behind-the-Green-Door. It is no breach of trust for me to say this, sir: Mr. Behind-the-Green-Door is less loyal to your Administration than to a previous one whose Chief Executive is preparing the grounds for a comeback.

The fate of RMS, I suspect, you know better than I, but it may interest you to know that when I interviewed him in Ulan Bator several weeks ago, he said, after reading these pages, that it would be a salutary thing for our nation, and he would raise no objection, if you were to make public the thoughts conveyed in the hand-obliterated segment of his July 20 letter to the President. Franklin Tompkins's resignation is another matter about which you must surely be the most informed, and I refer to him only incidentally to note that he is now living in New York's SoHo district, sharing an apartment with another former CIA agent, and that they are collaborating on a book about their experiences — in verse. More important, perhaps, is Nazim Aziz Tahir's resignation from the Istanbul police. I found him rather secretive about his present activities when I met him in a place I am obliged not to disclose. He was in relatively good humor, considering his disappointments, but asked to comment, he would say only, "I will get them."

Nick and Tony are alive and extremely well, sir. They are definitely neither in Greece nor in Turkey, and while they feel they have committed no wrongdoing, except, perhaps, pecuniary infractions in those two countries (where in any event no charges have been raised against them), you can understand their reluctance to reveal their whereabouts. All I can say further is that they have authorized me to state on their behalf that they have every intention to meet their tax obligation to the United States (which of course does not fall due until next April 15) — if on the advice of their many advisers it appears that such an obligation does indeed exist.

There is much I am free to report about the gold, however. On June 7, 1945, my research has revealed, the entire gold reserves of the German Reichsbank were stolen from a Nazi cache on Klausenkopf Mountain in Bavaria by a ring of U.S. military personnel and Europeans. They and their treasure vanished, and we now know why. History records this as the greatest robbery of all times, and probably the least enjoyed by the robbers. On August 19, 1977, a brokerage firm on the Bahnhofstrasse in Zurich negotiated the sale of 72,500 troy ounces of that gold (300 troy ounces of the 728 100-ounce ingots had previously been bartered by Nick and Tony, going a long way in securing their freedom of movement). The transaction brought $133.50 per ounce, driving the price down on the gold exchange that day by $.08, by the way. After expenses and commissions, Nick and Tony split $9,194,812.50, which they elected to take, in the first instance, in Swiss francs, German marks, Swedish crowns, Japanese yen, U.S. dollars, and approximately fifteen other convertible currencies.

Dobbs lives in a palace.

Sir, I have been to Ararat. Haunted by Tony's vision of what in a moment of great confusion and stress he saw as the remains of Noah's ark, I too, could not resist the call of the mountain. In exercising my profession, I have had occasion to travel over much of this planet, but in all humility I have never observed anything that can equal the mystical power of the Mother of the World. It rises on the plains like the only wall between heaven and earth, summoning, forbidding, at one and the same time.

I was neither prepared nor competent to climb the mountain, but I understood why others imperil their lives to do so, and still others refuse all trespass with a passion transmitted across the eons.

I have returned with no further news of the ark, Mr. President, only the words of a wise man — the Wise Man of Ararat. His name is Oo and he walks with a staff. He is old, but not ancient, and the nonjudging eyes of a child look out with their own light from the evident depth of his mind. I met him beneath a field of silver starlight so intense it cast shadows and illuminated the arêtes of the mountain. He simply appeared, sir. What I learned about him, that he is universally regarded by all who live in sight of the mountain as a Wise Man, that he has been there longer than anyone can recollect, I gathered from others afterward. There were no introductions, no questions asked of me or my purpose. This is all of what he told me, in a voice that lay against the moonless night like a diamond resting on velvet:

And now listen to what I am going to say. The Ark is still there! This I was told by the graybeards, and this they were told by those who were old during their time. And all of us here believe it. All the people of Igdir, of Bayazid, of Erivan, to the last shepherd on the twin mountains. But to reach it, the only way to reach it, is to be as pure as the newborn babe, free of every evil.

I looked up at the mountain. I don't mind telling you, sir,

especially you, I felt a rush of spiritual fear, something tangible and mighty but as delicate as the brush of an eyelash.

"Well," I said, not knowing what else to say, "that let's me out."

But he was gone.

Respectfully yours, etc.